Finding Tree Love

Monika Wiśniewska

FOR MY MAMA

Thank you for your unconditional love.
You are my best friend, my hope, my joy
and the most important person in my life
because you gave me life
to experience all the incredible things
which have taught me so much
that I can now share
a piece of my heart and soul
with the rest of the world.
You are true love.

Contents

Chapter 1

I AM A TREE

'If you've ever thought you had a bad day
imagine turning into a tree
and...
think again.'

\- Rupert

Once upon a time, in a kingdom far, far away, or maybe not that far, depending on where you are really, there lived a prince whose name was Rupert.

He was the only son to the King and Queen of Deer Wonderland Kingdom, where thousands of deer lived in the surrounding forest in peace and harmony, protecting their territory and females. The males had the biggest antlers imaginable, allowing them to scare off even the most dangerous predators. The deer were under the king's protection and anyone who would do any harm to them would be captured and put into prison for life. Nobody in the whole kingdom had therefore ever tried killing a deer, petrified of this severe punishment.

Prince Rupert, a rather handsome, dark-haired, and brown-eyed young man, had a kind and caring nature thanks to his parents' loving upbringing. He was, however, a bit temperamental and spoilt due to his various privileges from birth. He enjoyed riding his horse into the depths of Deer Wonderland forest where trees were tall, streams were flowing with crystal clear water, and animals such as hares, beavers, foxes, bears, birds, and of course deer, lived in perfect harmony. Rupert quite liked nature and one day he had an urge to venture out to the depths of the forest to test his new bow and arrows, the gifts that he had received from the king for his thirtieth birthday. The bow was gilded with golden eagles and the arrows were made of pure silver, shining in the sunlight. The king told him that the arrows should only be used when in mortal danger but on that warm and humid summer evening having noticed a perfect spot, Rupert decided to try it out. He got off his dark horse, pulled back the arrow in the bow, aimed at the old oak tree standing majestically on the other side of the stream, and just as he had let the arrow go, confident that it would hit right in the middle of it, a huge deer ran in front of it and stopped as if it grew into the ground, piercing Rupert's eyes with his huge, sparkling eyes. The deer's gigantic antlers were glowing with warm, blue light as if they were set on fire, which merged with the sky. A blue butterfly was flying around its head, glowing with a pulsating light of different shades of blue. Staring at Rupert, the deer did not move an inch, as if it knew that his death was inevitable and he was ready for it. In that split second, which seemed like an eternity for both of them, the silver arrow pierced the deer right into his heart and he fell on the ground with a big thump making his antlers stop glowing with the blue light and the butterfly fly away into the crowns of the trees.

Rupert was horrified, taking a big gasp of air. He would have never wanted to kill a deer, not in a million years. He felt great sadness and tears swelled up in his eyes. A moment later, his feet started to sink into the ground, as if he was now standing in the middle of a swamp, getting trapped in a muddy soil that turned solid once his ankles were buried into it. He was now unable to move. Looking in front of him, he saw an old man in a long brown cloak and a hood which was covering the majority of his long grey hair, holding a long, wooden stick, emerging from behind the trees. His pale, wrinkled face was expressionless and his cold, lifeless green eyes were fixed at Rupert's.

'Why did you kill the deer?' he asked without even blinking an eye, in a low but firm voice that could move a mountain.

'It was an accident, I'm sorry, I didn't mean to. I was aiming at the tree and the poor creature just ran in front of it. I would never kill a deer on purpose' Rupert quickly replied in a shaky voice, feeling guilty for what he had done.

'You will be punished for it,' the man replied in a voice that gave Rupert shivers through his body.

'Me?? Oh, no! You don't understand. I'm the king's son and I know my father very well. I know what the punishment for killing a deer is but he will not put me into prison because of this... little accident. He loves me and wants me to be the king when he dies' Rupert replied, gasping for air, feeling his pounding heart in his chest as if it wanted to jump out but he still tried to keep a brave face.

'The king is fair and he treats everyone in his kingdom the same way,' the man replied 'and therefore, you will be punished' the man continued with his statement, mercilessly.

'I will explain everything to him and he will understand. He is my father. He gave me this arrow for my birthday. He loves me and cares for me!!' Rupert exclaimed in a more desperate and pleading voice this time.

'You will not have a chance to explain it to him,' the man continued 'you shall stay here... forever!' the man added, making the word 'forever' sound as if it was the scariest word in the world.

'What do you mean... forever? Why? How?' exclaimed Rupert frantically but the old man swiftly turned around and disappeared behind the trees.

Unable to move his feet which were now stuck firmly in the ground, Rupert called for his horse.

'Helios, come here buddy, come closer, please! I can't move, can't you see? You need to come here and help me!' Rupert shouted but the strong wind started to move the leaves of all the surrounding trees and huge dark clouds covered the whole sky as if the night had suddenly fallen.

Rupert looked at his feet stuck in the ground which were now turning into long tree roots, quickly growing into the area around him and his legs turning into a massive tree trunk.

'Oh no! What's happening to me??? Help!!!??' he screamed in panic one last time before his whole body turned into a tall oak.

The branches were slowly getting covered in millions of green leaves and the roots were now stuck deep into the ground. Rupert opened his eyes, or rather two small cracks in the bark, and his heart sunk from despair.

'I am a tree??? Nooo!! That's impossible!! Oh God, this is only a bad dream and I'm going to wake up from it any minute. This is only a bad dream!!!' he exclaimed, stuttering in despair from a large brown huba, a crescent-shaped fungus, which was now his mouth. The smaller huba, just above his new mouth, became his nose.

'Oh no, I have no hands, no hands!' he exclaimed in horror when he tried to move but all that he could see was two of his biggest branches moving slowly, making a crackling and swooshing sound.

He then saw the same old man slowly emerge from behind the trees and stand right in front of him. He was accompanied by a group of giant spiders following him, which freaked Rupert out even more because he had never been fond of spiders, especially gigantic ones. The dark thick fog surrounded them now and the old man spoke again, having taken his hood off his silver hair.

'I told you that you will be punished. These are the ancient rules of the forest. The king does not need to punish anyone and put them in prison for killing a deer. It is only a myth. Forest Mother does justice for him and she is always fair and she is always right. She is more powerful than the king because she rules all the forests of the world. This is the unspoken rule which the king knows about and approves of. He respects nature because he knows its immeasurable and still undiscovered powers. Nature needs to be respected and deer cannot be killed just for fun. Especially Matras, the Deer King himself, the biggest and bravest leader of the herd. Now the forest needs a new leader and it's not going to be easy to replace such a strong, fair and wise deer. The herd will be without a good leader until a new one is selected in Deer Games, where the young and strong males will be fighting for the title and the privilege. You really don't know what you have done. Each action has its consequences and you need to bear yours now. It's called karma. God have mercy upon your soul and...well, good luck!' the old man said with a less scary but still a low and firm voice.

'I'm sorry, I really am, what else can I do? Where is she? That Forest Mother! I need to speak to her immediately! I will explain that it's all one big mistake! It was an accident and I wasn't hunting for fun! I'm sure that if I speak to her and explain it all, she will understand and forgive me' begged Rupert.

'Yes, of course, you can speak to her. She is everywhere. In the trees around you, in the river, in the air, she is in all the animals. You just need to find a way to communicate with her. There is only one way she will understand you.'

'What is the way? Tell me and I will do it!' Please, help me!'

'Unfortunately, you need to find the way yourself. There is no easy answer. If you do find the right way to speak to her, I'm sure she will forgive you and let you go back to being a human. But until you have learnt how the Universe works, you will be a tree, I am afraid.' the man replied putting the hood back on his silver hair and turning his back on Rupert again.

'Please don't leave me, please stay! Don't go! What do I do now? Please, tell me!' Rupert exclaimed but the man was already gone. The spiders followed his steps moving their huge hairy legs giving shivers to Rupert.

'Great, this is a disaster! It's a nightmare! What should I do? How?' he thought, scratching his head, or rather the crown of the tree with his largest branch acting now as his right hand.

The horse gazed at him with his big dark, shiny eyes, neighed loudly, showing off a set of white teeth, and galloped away into the depths of the forest.

'Wait! Where are you going?' Rupert screamed but Helios, just like the old man, disappeared from his sight, leaving him alone.

The strong wind stopped and the dark clouds moved away, revealing the scarlet glow of the sky at sunset, sprinkled with only a few pinkish fluffy clouds.

'Forest Mother! Where are you?,' Rupert screamed as loud as he could but heard no answer. 'I need to talk to you!' he screamed again but there was no reply and the only sound he could hear was the gentle and soothing sound of the stream, an owl, and birds singing in the distance.

'Hey, go away! This is not a place for you!,' he shouted angrily when a starling sat on one of his branches. He started to move rapidly, trying to scare the bird away but it stayed there as if it got stuck to him.

The bird then flew closer to him, touching him with his beak, as if searching for something in his bark.

'Hey, what are you doing? Stop! You are tickling me!- said Rupert, starting to twist left and right, trying to refrain from bursting out laughing from the unexpected sensation. The starling gazed at him with a surprised look, as if something was wrong with Rupert, and flew away.

'Oh God, this is a disaster, what am I going to do now? I can't live like this! I am a prince! A prince that will be a king one day.' he murmured to himself with a whining voice.

'Just relax and go with the flow!' he heard a low but soothing voice coming from another oak next to him.

'You can talk?' asked Rupert.

'Well you can talk too, what's so strange about it?' the oak replied, and having pulled his roots from the ground, he moved away making a swishing, whistling noise with the leaves.

'And you can move?? How? Trees don't move!!' Rupert exclaimed at witnessing this weirdness.

'Oh, relax, you can move too, just when you do, don't you dare follow me! I have enough of this noise of yours' the oak replied.

'I can move? And I can talk? Thank you, God! That means... that means... I can go back to the castle and ask my father for help' he thought, feeling sudden rays of hope with this revelation.

'You can go anywhere except the castle. That will never happen, so don't even try. Nobody can leave the Deer Wonderland Forest once you become part of it. Besides, Forest Mother will never let you ha!' the oak exclaimed joyfully from the distance before completely disappearing.

'Hey! I didn't say anything! You could hear my thoughts? I think I'm going to go crazy! Wait, I've already gone crazy! I'm a talking tree! And I can walk! I can walk? Really? Ok, let's see if that's true then.' he murmured.

'Ahhhrrrrr,' he moaned a few seconds later from the effort of trying to move his toes, or rather his roots.

'Come on, you can do this! Abracadabra! Move my feet! My roots, I mean!' he exclaimed to himself and the roots started to move whilst he was rocking backwards and forwards. After a while, they all came out to the surface.

'Yessss! Magic!' he said and laughed in the voice of an insane man who had just escaped an asylum.

'Now, let's walk!' he commanded in a firm voice as if he was leading an army to war.

'Urrrghhhh come on! Move!' he said with great effort, rocking side to side and moving inch by inch towards the river bank.

'Oh, no, not this way! I don't want to end up as a log drifting away with the river's current, now that would be unfortunate. Enough of unfortunate events for a day! I'm a blooming tree!' he thought and moved along the riverbank instead, gliding slowly on the ground. 'Oh, I mean an effing tree. The last thing I want is to have my handsome body covered in pink, fragrant flowers haha! he said to himself laughing out loud.

'Ok, that's enough for today. I'm tired now.' he said after what had seemed like an eternity but when he turned around, he realised he moved only a couple of feet away.

'Oh, I'm so tired, I think I'll just go to sleep now and when I wake up in the morning, I am sure this nightmare will be over.' he thought and closed his two cracks in the bark, his eyes.

'Stop it!' he shouted soon afterwards, having heard nothing but the cheerful singing of the birds.

The birds stopped but after a few moments, they started to sing sweet melodies again.

'I said, stop it!' he shouted again and one of the birds, a beautiful yellow one with a red tail and a beak flew closer to him.

'Why do you want us to stop? We are singing the latest songs from the Top Twenty of Deer Wonderland. They are the best songs out now. Don't you like them?' the bird chirped.

'You can talk too?'

'Yes and so can you' the bird replied adding; 'What's so strange about it? Where are you from? Have you been brought up with humans or something? Only they don't understand our language. They think we are just stupid birds, or at least, most of them think we are.'

'I don't care if they are the latest songs! I want to sleep. I am very tired now from talking, and walking. If you haven't noticed, I'm an old tree now! Tomorrow, I'll wake up from this horrible nightmare and be myself again!' replied Rupert.

'But you are yourself. Now. Even though you are a tree. It's still you, isn't it?' the bird replied happily.

'Well, yes. Well, no. Yes, it's still me but it's not my body. I'm a human being, a handsome prince with brown eyes and dark hair and a great muscular body. I am tall and very attractive. At least, that's what I heard many times from the ladies in court. Many princesses from other kingdoms dream of marrying me because I have so much to offer. A beautiful castle and chambers to live in, wardrobes full of silk dresses, gorgeous perfumes, lavish dinners, carriages to take them for rides, and, of course, beautiful diamond, ruby, and emerald rings. They send me lots of love letters daily hoping I will choose them as my wife and the new Princess of Deer Wonderland Kingdom. I am the most sought after prince you know!' said Rupert proudly, stretching his chest forward, or what was now the tree trunk. 'And I don't think you will understand it but I am also irresistible to women and an amazing lover. At least, that's what all the princesses I have made love to told me many times. They say I can even..'

'Woooow, ok no need to tell me details and I am sorry to break the news to you. It won't happen now! Your wealth, your carriages, your jewellery to impress them and your six-pack won't work any charm on them anymore' the bird replied laughing out loud with a thin squeaky voice and added; ' I don't want to sound horrible but as you have just said, you are an oak now, so forget about it. And when it comes to you being you and your personality, well it leaves some room for improvement, I dare say. You are not the most humble man, placing all your attention and value on the way you look and that you are rich because you have a rich father – the king. What else have you got to offer 'as you' though? Is your wealth all that you need to find true and everlasting love? Think about it, you will have plenty of time for reflections, ' the bird replied and shaped his beak into a cheeky crescent before stretching its colourful wings and flying away.

'Oh, that..., that... is not very nice! You little.... nasty bird, telling me what you think about me. How dare you tell me what you think. You don't know me at all. You think you know me because of a short conversation but you don't! And anyway, who voted for your songs? They are wishy-washy and not the top hits for sure' Rupert shouted angrily just as the bird had landed on a long branch of a tree right in front of him.

'But that's the reality and the sad truth that you need to face now. Think about it. Think about who YOU truly are. My advice to you is this; Accept what it is you have become. Surrender and don't try to fight it. It will only prolong your suffering. By accepting what is, you shall regain freedom, happiness, and even enlightenment. That's the only thing that shall save you. It is the key to salvation. Accept the present moment, as a tree. Trust me, I have seen it all before. Trees that accept who they truly are flourish and live happily for hundreds of years. Trees that cannot accept who they are dry out and eventually die alone, with broken branches.

'Oh, since when have you been such an expert on me and everyone else? You think you know everything but you don't.' replied Rupert defensively.

'And in my humble opinion, you need to finally learn what true love is because you still don't know despite your age.' The bird said in a way that seemed to Rupert as if it was a therapist talking to him and added 'Love is not just about being an amazing lover. You couldn't be further from the truth. You cannot see anything important with your eyes. Only with your heart.' the bird added.

'Is that so?' asked Rupert, amazed by the depth of this conversation.

'Yes, that's so. Also, for your information, it was the lady hares and ladybirds who voted for us! They love us and our songs and they are our biggest fans. Come on guys, let's go sing somewhere else, somewhere where our cute voices and efforts are appreciated. by the ladies, not by this one big moaning oak!' the bird replied and swiftly flew onto the other side of the river with other birds from his band, leaving Rupert in complete and utter silence.

'Finally! I can sleep now!' Rupert thought and closed his tired eyes descending into the darkness.

Chapter 2

ONE HUNDRED AND THIRTY YEARS YOUNG

'And when I awoke,
Warm sun rays penetrated every molecule of my leaves,
The energy rushed through my trunk
Making me thrilled and ecstatic about another day.
The sunrise, the biggest miracle of life on Earth,
Always leaves the darkness and gives new hope.
Hope for another day, for another chance,
To start all over,
To start again,
To turn my life around
And create a moment
That will never repeat itself.
Hence, the most precious thing in the world
Is the very moment
Each moment of life
That is unrepeatable
That is unique.
It cannot be bought.
It cannot be stored in a jar.

Only lingers in the air of eternal memories
Which connect us together
The universe and nature and every thought
The everlasting wisdom of the universe
The everlasting everything.
The only heritage we will give to our offspring.
Let's make sure each thought, each memory is worth passing on
As we want the world to grow and learn and contribute to its salvation
Not misery, hate, and suffering.
Let's clear our thoughts and minds.
Let's become the blank canvas to paint on
One thought at a time
Beauty in each
Wisdom in all
And reject any negative ones
As they only take us away from bliss.
The bliss that we all strive for
The joy we all yearn for
The love we all pray for
Let it become us'

- Rupert

When I woke up at sunrise, I felt warm sun rays touching my face. The air was crisp and fresh, filling my lungs and giving me energy. A couple of green birds with yellow wings started chirping in a happy voice and surprisingly, I didn't even find it annoying. The sun rising above the peaks of the trees was slowly turning from red to golden yellow, touching every leaf, every blade of grass on the meadows, and every mountain top at a distance. The castle on the hill was bathed in its golden rays, making it look young and fresh as if it was waking up from one thousand years of sleep.

'Thank God it was just a bad dream, I am myself again.' I thought to my relief ' but hey, how can I see the castle over the treetops? I don't remember being that.... tall!! Ahhhhhhhhh! I am still a tree! Oh, no! I am still a tree!' I exclaimed.

'Morning Rupert, did you sleep well?' asked a squirrel having flown to me from another tree, spreading her little legs like an orange kite, landing right on my nose and staring into my eyes with her big brown marbles.

'Ouch!!' I exclaimed, feeling a sharp pain from her sharp paws. 'You scared me! Don't do that again.' I said; 'Wait, but how do you know my name? And why are you on my nose?' I added.

'I know many things that you don't know! And since you are a tree, I can sit on you anywhere I like.' she replied in a squeaky voice, parting her lips and turning them into a crescent, showing off her tiny white teeth.

I knew it was a 'she' because of her fluffy ginger hair on top of her head which was styled into waves and she smelled of... lilacs. No male squirrel would smell of lilacs.

'So, did you sleep well?' she continued, moving around my trunk up and down, tickling me a bit but somehow I didn't mind it now.

'Yeah, I guess so, last night I hoped this nightmare would be over when I woke up but it looks like it was real. Do you know why I'm an ugly, old tree now?'

'You are not old and you are not that ugly. At least compared to this crooked one next to you. You are quite a handsome young oak, maybe only one hundred and thirty years old at my guess!' she replied while shaking her fluffy tail in front of my eyes.

'A hundred and thirty years old? Nooooo! I have just turned thirty and I am a young handsome prince! When I am a human, of course. I cannot be a hundred and thirty years old! This is getting worse minute by minute! It means, it means I should be dead now! Or maybe I am already dead now? Nobody lives that long!' I exclaimed.

'Oh, no, you are very young for an oak and in the tree world you are only a teenager, still very young, like you have just been born! Oaks can live hundreds of years and some say they can live forever. Can you see that guy over there? With big, thick, crooked branches? He is four hundred years old and he still has some energy to join us at dancing parties where we learn the foxtrot from the foxes! And I can tell you now, you are one of the most handsome young oaks I have ever seen and I have seen many!'

'How do you know my oak age anyway? How come you are so certain?' I asked, getting more and more curious.

'Well, I am an expert in trees. As you can see, I am a squirrel but we can check your exact age since you are so persistent.' she replied with a peculiar charm. 'Hey Julie, Malcolm, come! Let's see how old Rupert is!' she yelled and two other red squirrels ran down from the tree in front of me.

Having taken a vine of the tree nearby they wrapped my body with it and exclaimed simultaneously 'Yep, one hundred and thirty years old!'

'How can you be so sure?' I asked ' and from using just a piece of a vine?'

'For every inch around your waist you are one year old, so I'm sorry to break it to you. You are one hundred and thirty but as I said, that's nothing in oak living years, so don't worry.' She replied with a wide smile on her tiny face, showing off again her two front teeth gleaming in the morning sun.

'I see, well that makes sense, you seem to know your stuff. So what's your name?' I asked curiously as I had just learnt the names of two of her friends.

'My name is Leticia and I run the best 'Squirrel Knitting Club' in the whole forest. We make dresses made of moss, vines, and flowers, mainly for dra. . .' she suddenly stopped but added; 'If you would like to join our club, you will need to wait until next year because unfortunately, we don't accept any new members now. But I can let you know if we have any free spaces next Spring if you like?'

'No, thanks, I have never been a fan of knitting or making dresses. My mother made a cute little blanket for me when I was a baby and I de-knitted it beautifuly one day. That's the closest to this craft I have been to. But if you have a 'De-knitting Club for Oaks' I may join you next year.' I replied, chuckling at my incredible sense of humour. 'Oh, wait, I won't be here next year. What am I even joking about!' I murmured, chuckling at the very thought of me knitting as a tree. 'Leticia, umm that's a very nice name, but don't get me wrong as I don't want to sound rude. Who gave you your name? Surely squirrels don't have names.'

'Oh, it's Forest Mother who gave me that name when I was a baby. She came to my mum one day saying that from now on I will be called Leticia. My mum came here from another kingdom I forgot the name of, starting with an S.., met my dad and they stayed here. Anyway, I need to go now and look for the acorns I hid yesterday before I completely forget where I put them. Oh no, I think I have already forgotten where I put them, great! Another one bites the dust. There will be far too many new oak trees growing in this forest because of my sclerosis. I need to see Zelda, the fox hypnotherapist. I've heard she is quite good at helping other squirrels improve their memory and remember where they put their nuts. Especially useful for older male squirrels if you know what I mean... just kidding. Ok, well, have a nice day, and remember you are just a young oak. So no baby oak crying today, please! Bye!' she said and ran along my branch, right till the end of it.

'Hey wait, this Forest Mother, do you know her well? Where is she? I need to speak to her about this unfortunate mistake she's made!'

'Oh, yes, I know her very well. She is amazing and she never makes mistakes because she is perrrrfect. She is the one everyone respects and some are even scared of because her fury can be lethal. Everybody knows her. And everybody knows she should not be made angry because strange things can happen to them afterwards. So don't make her angry, that's my advice to you!' Leticia exclaimed and spread her arms and legs wide, flew in the air, and landed on the tree next to me.

She ran along its branches with the skill of a circus performer, twisting and turning around them with such flexibility that all I could say was; 'Wow, I wish I could do that. Why didn't Forest Mother turn me into a squirrel? I could be free and flexible like Leticia, and I could do what I want. Now I am an old but actually a young oak. True, I am tall so I can see over some of the treetops, and yes, supposedly I am handsome, for an oak of course, but that's it really. No princess will marry me now. Who would want to marry a tree? What am I going to do now? Where are you, Forest Mother? Where are you? I hate you for what you did to me. You are a horrible woman that punished me so severely for what was only... a mistake. This is the worst time of my life. Who would like to be a tree when they have their whole life in front of them? It is a punishment for which I will never forgive you, you nasty woman unless you immediately turn it back. Yes, you will have to do it and you will, as soon as I find you.' I said to myself in a feeling close to madness from being utterly powerless, imprisoned in a tree.

Chapter 3

ETHEREAL BEAUTY

Going for a walk when you are an oak is not an easy task. First of all, I am slow, secondly, I am heavy, thirdly my feet, since they are non-existent and are now a spider web of long roots, need to be dragged on the ground from left to right in a swaying motion, as if I am sweeping the floor. Yes, that's what it feels like to me even though I had never really swept the floor because that's what the servants did in the castle. Now I am an oak sweeper of the forest. The obstacles on the way don't seem to help either, the bushes, the gigantic ferns, the branches fallen from the trees, the weeds growing along the river. It's not like I am walking on the smooth surface of a frozen lake. But what else can I do? I just keep going. Despite the inconvenience of being a tree. I am not sure where I am going but I can't just stand there, grounded, and do nothing, waiting for my death. Especially if I am to live as an oak for another six hundred years or more! It's a long time to wait to die and do nothing with your time. I need to find the Forest Mother, this...this nasty woman who has nothing better to do with her time than turning a young and handsome prince into a tree. You wait till I find you and I will tell you what I think about your games and playing with people's lives. But I will do that only once you have removed the spell and I am free to be a human again. Before that, I will try to be nice to you...I will try. Oh, and... I need to stop talking to myself.'

Walking deeper into the forest after what had seemed like an eternity, I noticed a twinkling light behind the trees. I moved closer and closer. I came into an open space where a waterfall of crystal clear water gushing from the top of the rocks merged with the ripples of the turquoise surface of a lake surrounded by tall ferns. Colourful birds were scattered all over the treetops, chirping, singing, and tweeting, creating a harmonious melody as if an orchestra was playing a perfectly composed piece of music. The sun, high up to the west, was casting shadows of trees on the water surface. The powerful waterfall sprinkled the air with a mist of tiny droplets, gently touching my leaves, covering them all one by one. The scent of geranium and wildflowers was lingering in the air, surprisingly relaxing my 'tired from walking' body and stressed mind. Golden, pink and blue butterflies were dancing all around me, leaving behind them a tiny trail of sparkles every time the mist was touched by the sun rays, making the scenery look as if the whole forest was enchanted. Ummm, maybe it was?

'Wow, so this is what paradise looks like,' I thought with a big sigh and noticed a slim silhouette of a woman emerging from the ferns on the left side of the stream.

She seemed to be...completely naked, walking slowly into the crystal clear water whilst her long chestnut hair gently swayed on her bare back, wrapping the pearl-like skin of her shoulders, which seemed to be sparkling like diamonds, in sunrays. When her ankles were immersed in the lake, she lifted her arms into the sky and the water lifted itself on both sides joining her fingers and flowing effortlessly up and down, creating angel wings and the most beautiful vision I had ever seen in my life. The sculpted contours of her figure, her long legs, her long neck, and her back were twinkling in the mist all around her as if she was some kind of a forest goddess who could control nature around her. The rainbow appeared over the sky creating a dome for this divine spectacle. I knew she was out of this world. Her ethereal beauty made me forget for a split second about my misery of being a tree. After this most heavenly vision was over when she put her arms down, she turned around and looked straight into my eyes. I froze. She was the most beautiful woman I had ever encountered. Her dark, sparkling eyes pierced my soul to the core and I became breathless.

'Aukk, auk,' I started to choke, panicking that I would die in the most unfortunate moment, having seen the most stunning beauty on Earth.

She then took her eyes off me and jumped into the water, blending with the gentle ripples of the surface which were sparkling in the sun rays, as if turning it into liquid gold. I took a deep breath.

'Thank goodness, I can now breathe again' I thought. 'But where did she disappear? I can't see her,' I thought, when she descended under the water surface and my heart palpitations stopped. My heart began pounding fast in my chest. 'What if she needs help? I should just jump in and rescue her, she needs me.' I thought and just as I tried to dip my roots into the water which was pleasantly warm, I noticed her coming out on the other side of the lake with her wet hair stuck to her perfectly sculpted back, wrapping her feminine silhouette of a Greek goddess, but before I even blinked with my cranky wooden eyelids, she disappeared behind the gigantic ferns.

The sky turned into all shades of blue because the setting sun hid behind the rocks, turning everything into dark shaded forms. The blue butterflies seemed to have taken over the scenery because hundreds of them appeared from nowhere, swooshing their glowing blue wings in circles all around me and above the lake. This only lasted for a while at twilight, making me wonder if it was the most magical blue hour.

'Who was that? What an irresistible beauty... Surely she is an Angel sent from Heaven. How come I have never seen her before? I have been riding Helios in this forest ever since I was a child but I have never seen this waterfall and lake either. Strange. I guess I have never come that far.' I thought.

'If only I was myself, a handsome prince like I used to be, I am sure she would like me. I have no chance of impressing her now, being an ugly oak, with branches instead of my hands and a fungi huba as my mouth. She would never fall in love with me. Nobody would. Nobody would love a disgusting tree with nothing else to offer other than a piece of wood. I am nothing to her now. I am nothing to myself. I hate what I have become. I hate this new body. I hate this forest. I hate the horrible woman who did this to me. I hate this world. I will never accept who I am. Never. That bird knows nothing about me. He is wrong. I will change this. I will find Forest Mother and ask her for mercy. There is no other way for me to be happy again. I will find her and apologise for what I have done, even though I have nothing to apologise for. Killing that deer was only an accident and that's all I will admit to.

This nightmare needs to stop.

Now.

Chapter 4

QUACK

'Falling in love when you are a tree is more unfortunate than one may think because no human being will love you back' I thought in horror, resting my roots in a picturesque spot by the waterfall later that night.

'Who was she? I need to find her. What a beauty, what a woman. Where did she go? Where does she live? Why was she alone in the forest?' I continued my internal dialogue.

'That's Amara, the forest beauty, more beautiful than any other woman in the whole Deer Wonderland. Quack' said a voice from the middle of the bush in front of me, interrupting my stream of thoughts.

When I looked closer, I saw the most colourful duck I had ever seen in my life, with a red beak, white, blue, and purple stripes, reddish face and whiskers, and two large orange feathers that stood upright like sails of a boat in the sea.

'Who are you?' I asked.

'I'm Olek, your new friend, Quack!' the duck replied joyfully, shaping the beak into a crescent.

'I don't need friends, I am fine as I am. I just need to find Forest Mother and I will be done here, but I must admit you are very colourful for just a duck'

'I'm not just a duck. I'm a mandarin duck.'

'A mandarin duck? What's that? You like eating mandarins?' I replied, chuckling.

'My parents originally come from the kingdom in the East. Do you know where that is? Probably not. I was born in Deer Wonderland but as you can see I am proud of who I am. I love this forest but I dream of going back to the land of my ancestors and seeing where I come from! My mum and dad say we will all go there one day but at the moment they are caught up with many other things, such as getting another nest for my sister, you know what it's like in the forest, it's about location, location, location.'

'Oh, I seeeeee, so Olek, do you know where I can find that famous Forest Mother that everyone knows about except me? As you can see she played a horrible trick on me. I'm not who you think I am. My name is Rupert and I am a handsome, young prince, the son of your king. I just need to get rid of this horrible spell as soon as possible.'

'Umm, it's not as easy as you might think. You can't just go to her and tell her what to do. She will not like that. She is...umm how could I put it, a very strong and powerful woman. Nobody dares to tell her what to do. And that's because she already knows it all. She knows what you think and what you are about to say even before you do. Going to her and telling her what you want her to do will not work. But hey, that's just my opinion and who am I? Just a mandarin duck. Quack.'

'Ok, so what do you suggest then?' I asked, hoping I would finally get some clue into what I should do, even if it was to come from a... duck.

'Look, they are arguing again! Couples nowadays! Oi, stop it!' Olek exclaimed and flew to the other side of the stream towards two ducks making a lot of noise.

'Hey, wait, we haven't finished here! Tell me about Forest Mother!' I shouted but since Olek ignored me, I moved to the side to see what the commotion was all about.

'Where were you last night!? You filthy duck! I was waiting for you! I could hardly fall asleep because you just disappeared!' exclaimed a grey duck to a colourful one, looking at him as if she was about to bite his head off.

'I was with the other guys, Felix had his birthday party and we drank too much rose water which was very strong and seemed to be off, and then, we all fell asleep in each other's arms' the other duck replied trying to get through the noise of his partner.

'You could have called me! You could have sent Robin to let me know! You are such an egoist, not caring about my feelings! I really don't know why I married you! Quack,' the grey duck yelled back, turning her beak into a crescent pointing downwards.

'I'm sorry, but I need my freedom too, you can't just keep me in this prison. In this one pond only, unable to meet with other ducks and have some boogie-woogie. That's not the marriage I signed up for! Quack,' he shouted back.

'Ok, ok calm down everyone, I think I am getting a headache from your screams' I said finally, unable to listen to this noise anymore and at the same time wondering where my headache was actually coming from since I didn't have a...head anymore.

'Oh, Rupert, go away, it's a private matter. When you get married you will understand,' the colourful duck replied after a moment of silence.

'Well, that won't happen soon by the look of it! If you haven't noticed I'm an ugly tree right now!' I roared in anger and felt like bursting with tears but I stopped, thinking I didn't want to make a scene in front of complete strangers that I have just randomly met in a forest.

'Hey you are not ugly, you are a very handsome oak, quack,' the grey duck replied with a much softer voice which calmed my nerves.

'So you are married and you argue like this? Ok, so is this what marriage is about? Fighting like crazy ducks?' I asked.

'We got married at sunset four months ago. My good friend Rita the swan was the witness with her husband and we had a lovely party afterwards swimming in circles, laughing and eating lots of worms that they had brought for us. It was the most beautiful and happiest day of my life,' she replied with nostalgia in her voice.

'Oh, mine too,' her husband replied, gazing at her with watery eyes.

'Yes, Rita and her husband are swans and you see, they mate for life, so she can live peacefully, assured that he will not go after any other swan but this one here, well, there is no guarantee and he can easily get lost on the way home and end up somewhere in the nest of another lady mandarin duck,' she added, looking at Olek now and raising her eyebrows.

'Oh, no, no, no! My wife is faithful to me, I think you mean some other lady mandarin duck, please don't throw accusations without any proof. My beloved Nina and I are very happy right now and we are expecting ten babies. And they are all mine. Or at least I hope they are! Oh, I hate you now for raising your eyebrows without any proof. Don't do that again. Hopefully, they will all hatch but you never know with ducks. Maybe only eight or nine will. But we will be a family now and we are very happy,' Olek replied proudly.

'Ok, well maybe not with a mandarin duck then but I never know where this one is going to end up, just like last night, I was unable to sleep from stress and worry and he doesn't even care how he makes me feel,' she added, sobbing with big tears.

'Oh, my duckling, I love you and only you, I am sorry I didn't send my friend Robin to you with a reassuring message, carrying my feather as proof of my fidelity. Please forgive me, I will not do that again. I didn't know you would worry so much about me. You see I am still learning how to be a good husband and I need to stop thinking like a duck bachelor. I promise I will change for the better,' here, that's for you, please take it as my apology. Do you forgive me, my duckling?' he asked softly, smiling from ear to ear, holding the reed in his beak and flapping his eyelashes which seemed extremely long, at least for a male duck.

'Ok, I forgive you, dublidoo. But please don't do it again,' she replied firmly and took the reed from his beak. He then pinched her on the neck, nibbling on her feathers, making it red.

'Stop it,' she replied blushing and laughing through a half-open beak, trying to hold the gift she had just received and moving away because he now kept pinching her under both wings.

'Come, on, let's go home, I need some loooooove! Quack,' he exclaimed and followed her laughing and giggling, disappearing behind the reed.

'Wow, I think we have just helped a couple get all loved up again,' I said to Olek who was sitting on the edge of the stream watching the show with an open beak.

'Yes, we are a good team. I told you we will be good friends!' he replied with a smile.

'I don't need a friend. I am going to find Forest Mother and get the hell out of here,' I replied, moving away from him.

'Is this the way?' I asked Olek, who was just standing there as if he was stuck to the ground.

'I don't know. You don't want to be my friend so why should I tell you?' he replied and turned his feathery colourful bottom at me.

I set off alone into the darkest depths of the forest in the hope I would soon get to the very end of it. Passing the branches of other trees and stepping onto the rocks was not a pleasant experience. I guess trees were not meant to be walking, normally. But now that I have become one of them, this whole forest turned into a moving, talking place that I had never known existed when I was a human. I looked up and saw the sky turning into a darker shade of blue again. Reddish sun rays were now covering mine and other trees' leaves. I looked back and saw Olek walking behind me with his little feet.

'Hey, why are you following me? I told you I don't need friends!' I yelled.

'I think you could do with at least one friend here, you seemed to have scared all the birds already. What if you meet a wolf or a bear? Who will protect you then? At least I can help you with some advice,' he replied cheerfully.

'I don't need your help or protection. Why would a wolf or a bear want to attack an oak? And how could you fight a bear as a funny-coloured duck? Actually, I would like to see that! This is just a silly excuse to follow me,' I replied.

'You don't know what the wolves and bears are capable of once they realise you are a human in a tree. They may try to get to you, rip you into pieces and eat your flesh. And have you thought about trolls? They will cut you into pieces and use you as for the evening fire,' Olek replied in a growling voice which made me wonder if he was being truthful or just trying to scare me.

'Anyway, Olek, do you know where I can eat something? I have just realised I haven't had any food since yesterday when I turned into this..this..oh,' I replied, frustrated at the very thought of having lost my human form, my identity, and my handsome, sexy body.

'You're funny. You are eating all the time and you are drinking all the time. Through your roots and through your leaves, you are a tree now so that's how you live, you can't just have a deer steak and quail eggs for breakfast if that's what you want. But that's what you came here for anyway, right?' Olek replied with a voice filled with deep confidence of knowing all the answers.

'No I didn't come for that Olek, I already told you I didn't mean to kill that deer. So that means I don't need to look for food? At least that's handy, considering the circumstance of the unfortunate life I had found myself in. And no, I had never intended to eat that poor creature. I have already apologised to everyone. Why is nobody listening to me? Why is Forest Mother not listening to me since, as everyone here claims, she can hear me and she is everywhere,' I replied with a sigh that maybe it was not as bad as I had thought it was altogether but frustrated to be constantly accused of something I had never intended to do.

'Anyway, leave me alone now! I can take it from here. I shall find her on my own,' I shouted at Olek, getting annoyed by his loud quacks as if he knew all the answers in the world.

Chapter 5

TREE OF LIFE

Feeling a comforting warmth on my body, or to be more accurate my trunk, just as I was about to fall asleep, was not something I had expected to feel, alone in the middle of a forest. I also hoped it wasn't Olek getting cosy next to me like some weirdo duck. But then you never know with ducks like him. When I looked down, I froze. It was, it was...it was...her! The ethereal beauty! Her long dark hair was glistening in the moonlight while she was resting her back against me, reading a book by a little lantern with a candle in it. I could feel her energy emanating right through my wrinkled bark and up my spine, I mean, tree flesh, right up to the tips of my fingers, or leaves now. She was filling me with the most wonderful blissful feeling, making my juices flow really fast, something that I could only describe as... love.

'Oh dear, it's her and she is touching me. How do I let her know about my existence? I can't. She will never believe me that I am in fact a handsome prince. Oh, God. What should I do? What do I do?' I thought in panic.

I heard a rustling noise coming from the darkness of the surrounding ferns and then grunting and puffing. Before I even had a chance to say anything to warn my beauty, a giant beast covered in long silver fur with growling white teeth and vicious eyes jumped out of the bush, scaring my beauty who was now standing and leaning against me, having dropped her book and lantern lying flat on the ground. I could feel her breathing fast but she didn't say a word. The beast was moving closer and closer. I knew I had to defend her. I had to protect my beauty as she was about to die if I didn't. The beast, growling, with saliva dripping down its angry mouth, was moving closer, moving its huge paws towards us. The beauty did not move an inch, holding me tight with both arms, trying to hide behind me. I knew I had to do something. I lowered my branches and with full force, I hit the beast which flew high up in the air and fell on the ground with a loud thump. Lifting itself slowly, with the tongue dripping from blood from the cut on the side of its jaw, it retreated and ran away with a whistling sound from the ferns moving in all directions.

'Thank you for saving my life,' she whispered with the sweetest sounding voice, as if Heaven's harp was playing a welcome to Paradise.

I raised my branches and looked at her with amazement, wondering if she knew I was in the tree.

'Are you....ok?' I asked shyly, not knowing whether she would hear me.

'Yes, I am perfectly fine, I just got a bit scared. You see, that was Morteror, the night guardian of the forest. He often gets angry if he sees people wandering around at night. It's his time to rule and he protects his territory. But it was such a nice warm evening that I decided to come here and read my book, listening to the crickets chirping and frogs croaking,' she replied, looking straight into my eyes.

'Oh, I see, how come you are not afraid to walk alone in the forest? Especially at night?' I asked in amazement of her bravery.

'I live in the hut by the lake nearby. I have been brought up here. This forest is my home. I know everything about it. I am not scared of anything here. This whole forest is my home.'

'So don't you find it strange that I can talk to you? If you haven't noticed, I am a tree.'

'No, nothing will surprise me here. You see this forest is magical. It is full of things that many people haven't seen before. So a talking tree is not a surprise to me at all.' she said.

'Actually, I am not a tree, well I am, but in reality, I am a human being. I am Prince Rupert of Deer Wonderland Kingdom, the rightful heir to the throne. The castle on the hill is my home and that's where my mum and dad live, the king and queen. They must really worry about me, not knowing where I am right now. You see this wicked woman, called Forest Mother, turned me into this,..this..horrible oak tree only because I killed a deer.'

'So you are a man in this tree?' she asked.

'Yes, that's right. I am very handsome, with wavy dark hair and brown eyes, an amazing muscular body, and a six-pack. I am so handsome that all princesses from other kingdoms want to marry me,' I replied, proud of who I truly was.

'I see. A handsome prince in a tree. You know, I may look like I am just a naive young girl but I don't believe it. Actually, I have never heard of a more ridiculous story,' she replied, chuckling.

'But it's true! I am a handsome prince in this..in this tree! You have to believe me!' I replied, feeling my blood in veins or juices in my trunk boiling up.

'Well, I know trees can talk but I didn't know they had such an imagination. I suggest you see the doctor, Zelda, the lady fox who can cure any tree illness, even the ones which are, you know...imaginary,' she whispered and blinked with a cheeky smile.

'Thanks for the advice but I am not crazy! I am just a tree! That's all! No, I mean, I am a prince! Awwwhhh I am losing it now, I am losing my identity! Who am I???' I exclaimed in frustration.

'Ok, ok, calm down. Even if I believed you, what would that change?' she replied in a more serious and calm voice.

'Well, for a start, you can tell me where to find the horrible woman who did this to me.'

'And who is that woman?' she asked with curiosity.

'The old man said her name is Forest Mother, do you know her?'

'What old man?'

'When I killed the deer, a huge majestic one with antlers glowing as if they were on blue fire, he showed up and with a fierce voice announced I would be punished and that only Forest Mother can take this spell off me,' I explained as well as I could.

'Oh that could have been Tallin, the forest guide, he lives in the forest, not far from me and his job is to make sure everything works perfectly well. I was brought up by him after my parents died shortly after I was born. He often visited me offering help. I don't want to sound horrible, but you kind of deserved your fate for killing a deer. Why did you kill the poor creature?' she asked.

'I didn't mean to kill him, it was an accident, he ran in front of the silver arrow that I had aimed at the tree, I only wanted to try the birthday present from my father.'

'Ummm, you shouldn't have aimed at the tree. What tree was it?'

'It was the tallest tree I have ever seen, much taller than all the others and it was wide and strong and I thought it would be ok to fire the arrow at it.'

'The Tree of Life!? You tried to hurt the Tree of Life? No wonder you have been punished so severely! It is the tree that all the other trees are connected to. If anything happens to that tree, the whole forest would get sick and soon die. Nobody can harm that tree, not even with an arrow. This wound could get infected and the tree would die. Forest Mother must have sent the poor innocent deer to sacrifice its life in order to protect the whole forest. So now you killed the King of the Deer herd and they are left without the leader. So..., so... inconsiderate of you. No wonder you were so severely punished for this sacrifice and I hope you have learnt your lesson,' she replied,

'Oh dear, that's truly terrible about the deer and the tree, I..I.. didn't know all that. Can you see what I just did? Dear deer?' I replied with a sneaky smile trying to lighten up the conversation.

'Of course, you didn't know and you didn't care because you are just an egotistical human who thinks he can come to the forest and do any harm to it without any consequences,' she replied, moving slightly away from me.

'Hey, you are a human too, right?' I asked, trying to point out the obvious so maybe she would stop judging me.

'The difference between you and I is that I love this forest more than anything and I would die to protect it. All you did was to cause the death of the one who had lived here peacefully,' she replied in a firm voice, lifted her lantern, closed the open book with an oak leaf to mark where she had stopped reading it, and ran into the darkness, leaving me all alone again.

'Ohh she is amazing. What a woman! So outspoken, so temperamental but so caring. What has just happened here? She told off an oak and left?' I thought.

Chapter 6

INVISIBLE

Hearing horns in the distance only meant one thing to Rupert, that the rescue is on its way and he will soon be saved from his tree imprisonment.

'What's that?' asked Olek who jumped on one of Rupert's branches.

'That must be..my rescue. I recognise the horns. My father, the king himself, is coming to save me! Thank goodness miracles do happen after all. I just need to help him find me here,' he replied but as much as he had wanted to get his roots out and move in the direction of the sound, he couldn't.

'Why can't I move? I need to find my father so he can take me away from here.'

'Um they are getting closer. I think you can't move because they are humans and you can't let them know about your exis-tence. Not as a walking and talking tree, at least,' Olek replied and just as he had finished, two hunting dogs jumped out of the bushes in front of them, followed by three royal horsemen blowing horns.

Next came the king, dressed in his leather jacket, wearing a suede green hat with a feather. He stopped, looked around, lifted his arm, and exclaimed; Stooop! We need to take a rest, let the horses drink from the river, they must be tired.'

'Yes my, Lord' the king's court man confirmed and jumped off his horse, walked up to the king, and helped him get off his black stallion.

'Father, father! I am here!! I am so happy you found me!! I have been waiting for you for so long!!' Rupert exclaimed but Olek replied, 'I told you he can't hear you, he is a human, you can't communicate with them.'

'I can talk to them! I can talk to Amara! She is a human!' Rupert replied with confidence, not letting Olek distract him from his mission. 'Father, father, I am here!' he shouted even louder but Olek said, 'Shhh, my ears will explode in a minute. He can't hear you! Don't you understand?' he added.

'But why? Why? He is here, to rescue me,' Rupert replied, unable to move, paralysed from roots to the top, 'why can't you hear me! I am here, father!' Rupert wept inside but no tears could flow from his wooden eyes.

'I think we need to get back, it's too late to continue our search. It's getting dark and a big storm is coming from the west,' the king said to his court man on the right. 'Where is he? It's been days since Rupert was gone and I just don't understand why he would let his horse come back to the castle on its own. Something bad must have happened. Where is my beloved son?' he continued.

'Wait, what's that?' he asked, having noticed a shining object in the fern.

He moved closer and saw the bow that he had given Rupert as his birthday present.

'Look, Lord Thomas, that's my son's bow! My gift to him, he was carrying it the last time I saw him going for a ride. He must be somewhere here. I hope nothing bad happened to him. My dearest son. Where are you!?' he exclaimed with desperation.

'I am here!! I am here, father!' Rupert cried out once more but in vain. The king walked up to Rupert.

'Please, get closer to me father, maybe then you can hear me!' whispered Rupert and just then, as if the king had heard him, he placed his left hand on the bark and covered his eyes with his right hand, wiping his tears away.

'I am here father, I love you and I miss you and my mother, please hear me, please save me from this misery, I am here,' he whispered and felt so sad that a drop of water squeezed from his leaf travelled down to his father's hand, touching it gently.

The king lifted his eyes and felt the drop on his hand.'Yes, father, I am here, it's me Rupert' he whispered in despair but received no response, feeling the most excruciating pain to be so close to the one he loved and who couldn't feel or know about it. How could I be so close and unable to express my love?' he thought.

The king removed his hand from the bark and at a fast pace mounted his horse and exclaimed, 'Let's go! It's time!' And just like so many before him, he disappeared into the darkness of the forest.

Rupert was staring at the disappearing silhouettes of the people he knew and his beloved father. Once more, he was left on his own in the darkness of his own soul thinking; 'I am invisible. Why me?'

Chapter 7

TROLLS

'Amara, catch!' woofed Runo, a human-size silver-grey wolf with a white heart on the left side of his muscular body, as soon as he had jumped out of the bunch of tall ferns.

'Whaaaat's this?' exclaimed Amara when she caught a giant ball made of wet moss. 'What are you doing?' she asked.

'Let's play!' replied Runo with a smirk, showing off his giant sparkling white teeth and pointing his long ears towards each other, folding them one on top of the other creating a little bow, just like he did every time he wanted to play or he begged for mercy for being naughty.

He then jumped towards Amara trying to catch the ball with his teeth but Amara, having realised this was going to get funny, lifted the ball high up in the air, avoiding his teeth sinking into it...just. She threw it high up in the air and when it was falling down she hit it forwards with her arm. 'Ouch!' she exclaimed because she hadn't realised how tough it was going to be. 'What do I need to do to win?' she asked and laughed, having started to chase the ball right next to Runo who turned around the tree as soon as he had seen that and ran after her and the ball.

'Well, can you see the two branches up there? You need to get the ball stuck in between them if you want to win but you won't because I will!' replied Runo laughing out loud but as soon as he had said it, he ended up flattened on the oak, sliding down like a pancake from a frying pan.

'Oh dear, I think I may win after all!' exclaimed Amara, catching the ball and throwing it right into the middle of the two branches.

Runo, having quickly recovered from his embarrassing moment, jumped high up in the air and hit the ball with his head, saving the score at the last minute.

'You clever beast!' shouted Amara and ran after the ball again but as soon as she had caught it, she stopped as if she had become stuck in the ground.

Two giant trolls stood right in front of her. Staring at her with their big, dark evil eyes they lifted her by her arms. She dropped the moss ball and screamed, 'Runo!!'

In the moment that followed there was only a whirlpool of wind and a swishing sound. When she opened her eyes again, she was already on Runo's back, holding him by the soft white fur on his wide neck, feeling the strong wind in her hair caressing her cheeks and brushing her long hair, seeing nothing but the tops of the trees and the sun setting on the horizon, getting ready to be tucked into sleep by the big fluffy clouds.

'Thank you for saving me again. What would I do without you? You are my best friend. A friend I have dreamt of my whole life! Thank you for always being by my side. I love you so much!' she said, caressing his long fur on his back and lying her head on his neck.

Runo kept running with an incredible speed, getting higher and higher, hardly touching the crowns of the trees. He was silent and only feeling great love and gratitude for Amara's friendship too. Maybe because he was a male wolf it was more difficult for him to communicate his feelings to her, or maybe because love didn't require many words anyway. He knew how to show it to her with every molecule and every hair of his silver-grey fur. He also knew that his white heart on his fur was the second heart only for her.

'Let's rest here,' he said finally, having jumped on the tall rock by the waterfall, shaped like the palm of a hand facing up. The water was gushing steadily making a gentle noise which he thought would make the whole experience a bit more relaxing now.

'What do they want from me? Why do they always want to catch me and why do they want to hurt me?' asked Amara looking at the tired but 'sparkling from the sunset' eyes of Runo.

'I think they just want to hurt you because..well you are you and they will never be like you. You are beautiful and you are loving and compassionate. You know how to talk to the whole forest and for me, you are the Queen of the Forest if I may say so, not Forest Mother' he replied, stretching his paws on the warm rocks, feeling a sense of achievement after the successful escape from danger.

'But why do they feel this way? Why can't they be like me? Love nature, love the trees, and love animals? It doesn't take much to show love to the whole Universe, it's the biggest joy we can experience here on Earth. Why else would we be born into this world and not feel this incredible love for it? They can do it too, I am sure. Why does nobody teach them how to live a better life? Maybe they just need help?'

'I don't think anyone would dare to try to help them, they would eat them alive before they even had a chance to do some counselling on them. You know, they go back to their caves each evening and sit there by the fire, alone or in small groups, unhappy about another day, unhappy about another night, feeling angry and hateful towards themselves and the whole world. They are beyond getting any help. I tried. Once. It didn't end well. I had to run quicker than I did with you just now. Until they learn to love themselves first, nothing and nobody will help them. They may not be as pretty as you but they have their own troll beauty. Big fluffy ears, bellies, hairy feet, and round red noses. If they were nice inside, people would see them as the cutest forest creatures ever. I am sure of that, but as I said, they hate who they are inside and out, hence they express their hatred towards others too by wanting to kill them and then fry them for supper. Universe helps them and us but until they learn to love and accept themselves for who they are, we will live in mortal danger forever.

'This is very sad Runo but you know what, I believe that one day they will learn about the power of love. They will find it within themselves and this world will be a better place. Call me a dreamer..but I do truly believe that,' replied Amara with strengthened passion in her voice and enthusiasm.

'You know what Amara, call me crazy but I think you may be right. One day, a miracle will happen and trolls will be cured of their hatred. And I even know who will help them with that'

'Who?'

'Let's go and get some dinner. I noticed some juicy berries by the river bank as we were passing,' replied Runo, changing the subject and offering Amara his big strong paw so that she could climb on his back again and go for another ride.

Chapter 8

CRADLE

Being one of the tallest trees in the forest has its advantages such as waking up to the beautiful sunrise which I can admire from above the other trees and watching the morning mist slowly lifting from the valleys.

In moments like this, I forget about my miserable life of being a tree. Also, moments I spend with Amara make the whole experience somewhat nicer.

'I really like her, I really do like her. I can't wait to be myself again and be able to tell her how I feel about her,' I said to myself, deeply inhaling fresh air and hearing my new friend Robin starting his morning sonata.

'Hey Robin, how are you today?'

'I am happy as always. I think you can hear it in my voice? Even though I have a bit of a sore throat today and my vocal cords are a bit cranky this morning.'

'Oh no it's fine, you sound good to me.'

'Whooooahha. You have actually paid me a compliment? You are actually turning out to be...a nice oak' he said.

'Well, no point in being horrible to each other since we have to be here..for now at least, but not for long, remember,' I replied.

'Why are you so happy? Is it because of that...girl?' he asked with a cheeky smile on his beak.

'Maybe, no,...or maybe yes..., I don't know. I really like her, you know. I think I fell in love,' I replied.

'Yes, I can see that, your bark gets red every time she gets closer. Does she speed your pulse up with her presence? And does she give you butterflies in your stomach?'

'Oh yes, she makes my pulse go crazy, I mean, I don't have a pulse now, or maybe I do? And butterflies? Maybe they don't show up in my stomach but they do show up every time she is close to me. Lovely blue ones radiating with a pulsating blue light. But I admit, I am so confused. I just need to find this Forest Mother. Have you heard anything about her and do you know where she can be found?' I asked.

'Nope, not really, I will ask the badgers when I visit them today. But I can't promise anything. They are about to have some babies you know? They are organising a baby shower. Do you want to come?' asked Robin invitingly.

'Umm don't you think I would be a bit too big to attend a baby shower?'

'Oh, no, you will be fine. Ok, maybe a little too big but you can just stand at a distance. Mama badger Emily has already mentioned she would like to meet you. They are a very nice couple but Tommy, her husband, likes to party a lot. I will tell you in secret though; he is very nice and well behaved when he is with her. You know what I mean? Anyway, do you think they will have five, six or seven babies? What's your bet?'

'Oh, how should I know? I am not exactly an expert in babies. Ok, I will go with you, anything to distract me from standing here like a log all day. When are we going?'

'Well, considering the speed you move at, we had better go now. Maybe we will get there for afternoon tea. What shall we take as a present? Any ideas?'

'Oh Robin, seriously? You are asking me?'

'Ok, ok, I have an idea. Let's take some lilies for Emily and for the little ones...ummm. How about you make a baby cradle from one of your branches? That would make it a very personal gift. Can you do that? I will get some fresh moss to make it soft for them and bluebells to make it pretty.

'Ok, let me try,' I replied, and seeing Robin fly away to get some moss I picked the little branches lying next to me, still wet from the morning dew, and shaped them into a small basket. Cutting off my own branch would be barbarian.

When Robin came back we put the soft fluffy moss inside and I reached out for a couple of lilies from the water and attached them to the opposite side of the basket. Robin then picked a few bluebells and sprinkled them all over the cradle.

'There you go,' I said, 'Happy now?'

'Well, well, well, I must say Rupert you have got talent and when you have your own babies you will be a good father making cradles from branches and stuff...very nice my friend!' said Robin sticking out his orange belly forward and shaking his big grey fringe which looked like a haircut of a peasant, but I never dared to tell him that right in his beak, not wanting to hurt his feelings.

'Hey don't push it, I am far from thinking about babies, yet. I am still young, only thirty, I have time.'

'I wouldn't exactly say that...you are about a hundr...'

'Stop it, it's only a temporary glitch. It will all be over soon,' I replied and lifted the cradle, the sweetest thing I have ever created in my life, and started to move, slowly, as usual.

'Which way?' I exclaimed.

'Follow me. And if you don't mind, I will continue with my morning song as you kind of interrupted my routine,' said Robin flying right in front of my nose.

'Ok my friend, no problem.' I replied and with slow swooshy movements, I started to glide on the wet leaves and conkers. 'If you could just remove your feathery bottom from right in front of my face that would be great' I added.

When we finally got to the side of the river, which indeed took us a while, mama badger was so excited to see us she ran out of her house, a little wooden hut, covered from roof to the ground with moss, with only a tiny little window with wooden shutters, and ran towards Robin and me to welcome us.

'I am so happy to see you! Please come in, I mean except you Rupert, obviously, it's nice to meet you! I have heard a lot about you!' she exclaimed in a warm feminine voice.

'Oh really? I hope only good things?' I asked.

'Oh no, quite the contrary. I heard that you are moody, annoying, moaning all the time and that you hate being an oak,' she replied with a sweet badger smile showing off her two white teeth with a wide space between them.

'Umm, it's good to know, and who told you that?' I asked, staring at Robin who pretended to be whistling and rushing to get into the hut with his tiny feet which only meant that he was the traitor.

'Oh, don't worry, I can imagine it's a big change for you from being a human but trust me, soon you will absolutely love being an oak and you will want to be one forever,' replied Emily.

'Oh no, I am certain I will not want to be an oak forever, I can guarantee you that.'

'Umm yes, sure, we will talk about it later. Now stay where you are and I will bring you some...umm would you prefer smoked conkers or dried nuts?' she asked.

'I am not a squirrel you know, so thank you. I am fine as I am. I get all the food and drink from the Universe now.'

'Hey, you called for a squirrel?' asked Leticia, landing from the tree nearby straight into the cradle.

'How lovely to see you. Yes we were just talking about food with Rupert,' replied Emily.

'Oh talking about... food, I do need to see the fox therapist next week, even though she is currently very busy counselling all the squirrels who forgot where they put their nuts.'

'Why, what happened?'

'Oh well, I heard Olek talking to his ducklings the other day and he said to them; You are what you eat.'

'What does it mean?' asked Emily confused.

'It means... I am nuts! That's all I eat!' replied Leticia and jumped out of the cradle, making me confused by the confession and wondering if I was nuts too because after all I was also full of nuts. Maybe I was nuts too?

'I wonder where she is,' said Emily looking around as if confused.

'Are we waiting for someone?' I asked.

'Yes, my best friend Kitty was also supposed to show up but I think she must have been caught up with the others finishing work on the river dam,' she replied.

'Who is Kitty?' I whispered to Robin.

'Oh don't you know that her best friend is a beaver? Everyone in the forest knows her because she is great fun. Emily loves playing with Kitty the Beaver in her free time,' he replied.

'Kitty the Beaver…this forest will never cease to amaze me' I whispered back.

'Anyway, here Emily, this is a cradle for the babies, ready for Spring,' I replied, handing the gift to mama badger whose eyes were instantly filled with bulky tears.

'This is.. this is..wonderful! Oh, thank you so much Rupert, that's exactly what I was dreaming about! Look darling! That's what I was talking to you about when I said I want a baby cradle!' she replied and took her husband's paw who was standing at a distance, pulling him towards it.

'Yes, I can see that my dear, well you wanted it so now you have it. Sorted!' he replied in a cold voice.

'What I meant was that I wanted it for you to make one like this…but you always complained you didn't have time. You said you had to build a latrine for our neighbour and then make more tunnels for these cheeky moles. I am always the last one for you. Always at the end of the queue,' said Emily disappointed.

'Oh stop it, my dear, you know it's not true, I have to work to provide for you and the babies, you know how much I love you,' he replied, kissing her paw gently, making her blush on her white stripes in her face and winking at me with his big, brown, excited eyes.

'It was Robin's idea to make a cradle, I just wanted to help,' I replied, seeing Robin flying around dressed in a flower crown on his huge messy fringe, sipping from a big bowl and singing loudly.

'Oh Robin, this is too kind of you, please try the punch but just be careful as it's made with local grape juice and we have had it for a while so it may be a bit off,' said Emily.

'Grape juice?' he asked and burped, having taken another huge sip, swaying to the sides in a zigzag motion, 'Oh quack! I think I may have gotten a bit drunk,' he added with the sleek, smooth, and low-sounding voice of a drunken bird, collapsing flat on the riverbank stretching his wings and tiny legs to the side.

'I love you,' he mumbled and fell into a deep sleep, snoring like a bear.

'How embarrassing,' I thought, looking at Emily who only smiled, 'especially since it was his idea to come.'

Chapter 9

STAR

As soon as I had returned back to my usual spot by the river, I started to look for Amara.

It was already dark and the wind had stopped, giving way to a gentle breeze and fresh air that filled my lungs, or what used to be my lungs...anyway. I stood at 'my home' or the spot which I considered to be my 'home' since I had turned into the tree and I found it kind of comforting. I noticed a light at a distance. 'I hope it's her,' I thought, and a few moments later there she was, my beauty, emerging from the shadows of the forest holding a lantern in one hand, giving her a warm, candle-lit glow on her sweet face. Her eyes sparkled when she noticed me, probably because I was staring at her with my huba mouth open. She was the most beautiful, stunning woman I had ever seen in my life. Her long hair was gently touching her shoulders and the light blue dress, stunningly cradled her bare neck and décolleté as if it was the most precious crown jewel on a queen herself. It's just she didn't need any jewels. Her natural radiance was all that she needed to glow with the un-earthly beauty on this Earth. 'If only she knew how beautiful she was. If only she knew how much I liked her.'

'Ummm, are you going to just stand there and stare at me Rupert,' I heard her asking, waking me up from the dream I was experiencing.

'Well, what else can I do? I am only a tree, after all, remember?' I replied, hoping she would laugh, and she did chuckle at my first attempt to joke at my unfortunate position.

'Where were you all day? I was here earlier today and you were just gone. You don't obviously just stand here all day, do you? Did you go for a walk?' she asked with a gentle smile getting closer to me.

'Oh, yes I went with Robin to the mama badger's baby shower. You know they are going to have at least twins if not triplets or quadruplets or just ten of them, who knows, so I made the baby cradle with fresh moss for them and they really liked it. But Robin got a bit tipsy from the grape punch. He stayed there as he couldn't walk or fly, actually, he looked like a drunk kite when he tried, so I asked Emily to let him stay overnight. He was also quacking all the time which I find bizarre because he isn't even a duck.'

'It looks like you had fun,' she replied and sat down on the big stone and put the lantern next to her feet.

'You look...very nice tonight...are you going somewhere?' I finally asked, trying to break the awkward silence.

'I came here. To see you,' she replied quietly.

'Ohhh umm,' I mumbled, not knowing what to say. If I could blush, I probably would have but that's one good thing about being a tree, you just can't blush if your skin is actually the bark.

'Look, the first star in the sky just showed up. It's Sirius, also known as the 'Dog Star' , the brightest star we can see at this time of year,' I finally said.

'Where? I can't see anything. You are covering the whole sky with your big branches....'

'I am so sorry, how about I lift you up to the very top and you can see it from there?' I offered, surprised by my own inventiveness.

'Oh, ok, sure, but is it safe? Won't you drop me?' she replied, clearly worried about my tree lifting skills.

'Don't you worry my dear, I am a very skilled oak. Watch!' I replied and lifted her gently with one of my branches from the ground and made sure she wouldn't be hurt by any of the leaves on the way up. I made space for her, moving all the branches away and placing her on the very top of my crown.

'Wooohooo! This is amazing!' she exclaimed, smiling and laughing!

'You like...?' I asked, thrilled to see her so happy.

'I love it, It's unbelievable! And I can see the whole forest, the valley and even the castle! Oh sorry, I didn't want to remind you of it. Silly of me,' she replied.

'It's ok, I can see it too, day and night. It gives me hope that one day I will return home, to all the people I love, to my mum and dad who must worry about me every day.'

'You are very lucky, though, you can be so close to the sky! And see the stars and the Moon so close every night. I wish I was so tall,' she replied, trying to comfort me.

'Well, if you were so tall you would be a giant and I am not sure you would like that. Imagine how big your dress would need to be. It would take months to make. And the shoes. I won't even go there, women with big feet were never my thing,' I replied, chuckling at my sense of oak humour.

'Thanks, Rupert, I get it. Anyway, what's that star there?' she asked, pointing with her finger right up in the air.

'That's not a star, that's Planet Venus, but it's very bright right now so it seems like a star,' I replied with confidence.

'How do you know all these things? I mean, you do know a lot about nature and the Universe.'

'I don't know actually, I didn't know about it all before I turned into a tree. My father taught me a lot about the world but he didn't know as much as I know now. It's strange because as soon as I have a question about something I get an answer. It's like I am interconnected to an infinite knowledge of the Universe which gives me all the answers I need. The only answer I haven't received yet is how to go back into being a human again which is my biggest dream.'

'Is that your biggest dream?' she whispered leaving her lips slightly open as if waiting for my answer.

'Yes..I guess so, I mean what else am I to dream about now? When I was a human, the handsome young prince, I had other dreams too. I dreamt about conquering the world, helping my father keep the peace and happiness of our people. I wanted to take part in battles with enemies and show I am worthy of becoming King one day. I wanted to gather wealth and recognition for our kingdom, and of course, I wanted to marry a beautiful princess...and start a family,' I explained.

'A princess? Did you have any candidates?' she asked, with a small hesitation in her voice.

'Yes, there were a couple that had been invited to the ball last summer and I quite liked them but I couldn't get a deep connection with them. All they wanted to talk about was how many horses I have and what jewels they would be allowed to wear from the family treasury once we got married. It was all a bit..well..'

'Superficial?' Amara finished my sentence as if she could read my mind.

'Yes, exactly that, superficial and I really wanted to find true love.'

'Umm, don't get me wrong but you also talk about wealth and materialistic things too. Maybe they thought that's what you expected anyway. So you haven't found true love yet?' she asked, squeezing the branch she was sitting on as if with anticipation to my answer.

'Well, no,' I replied but with hesitation as if it was not true anymore, as if I had already found true love...in her but I couldn't tell her that, it wouldn't be appropriate and God knows what she would have thought about me, silly oak professing love to her whilst looking at the stars. I knew I had to turn into my handsome human self to be able to tell her that.

'I like you, Rupert, even though you are a tree!' she said as if she could hear my thoughts.

'Oh, I like you too Amara, very much so,' I replied, not sure if what I had just heard was my imagination or not.

'I think you are a good oak. I think you will find true love and be happy one day. But I also think you have a lot to learn about yourself, the universe, and love itself before you can find true love with a woman'

'Oh, you think so? I..hope I can find true love in a wonderful woman who will love me as much as I love her. I have been hoping for it for many years, which sometimes seems like an eternity because I think that to love and to be loved is the most wonderful thing on Earth. Right after winning wars and other such things...just kidding,' I replied giggling at my sense of humour.

'I wish. . .' she said.

'You wish for what?'

'I wish I had a star from the sky, just one. I could take it home with me and it would brighten up the sky right above my house at night. I could look at it through the bedroom window and she would be my little ray of hope, that one day, I will also find true love. Just like you hope for it. You know...it's also my biggest dream. To find the man who will love me as much as I love him. Forever and ever. I have also hoped to meet him for a very long time but all the men around me are just stupid. All they care about is how many acres of land I have inherited after my parents' death and how much it's worth now. I just don't want to marry any of them when I hear that,' she replied.

'I know exactly how you feel. I feel the same way. Listen, if you like I can ask the Sky if I can give you one of its stars. Would you like that?' I offered, knowing that now I can communicate with anything and anyone in the Universe.

'Really? Are you sure? You can ask the Sky? But how?' she exclaimed, excited.

'Wait, give me a minute, I need to close my eyes,' I replied, knowing I needed to connect to the Sky with an invisible communication channel that was not the same as a human language.

Amara stopped wiggling from the excitement on the branch, went dead quiet, and waited in anticipation. When I opened my eyes, she was grabbing my leaves from excitement, wanting to know what I was about to say.

'That's...' I started.

'What did the Sky say? Tell me? It's ok if it didn't agree, I mean it's a huge wish and I know I'm asking for a lot,' she said, not even letting me finish my sentence.

Without saying a word, I stretched my longest branch right up into the middle of the darkness of the Sky because somehow it went as far up as to touch the tiny little star right above us. I grabbed it gently and pulled it down.

'That's for you. A star from the Sky. As you have wished for it my lady,' I said, handing the shiny little ball of sparkle to Amara. 'Here, it's for you, The Sky agreed. You can keep it, but you need to look after it from now on. And there is one condition. You cannot keep it inside the house. That's not where the stars belong. It would soon die missing its home, the Sky. But you can let it float right above your hut. It will guard you each night and send loving energy to you and everyone surrounding you. At least, that's what I have just been told.'

'Really? Oh thank you so much Rupert, I l...' she stopped as if she was going to say she..loved me but most likely just liked me.

'I love it, thank you,' she finished, holding the little star in her hands, making her eyes sparkle like little stars themselves.

She looked so happy and radiant. I was so happy I could do it for her. After all, it's not a lot. I wish I could do more to show her how much I cared for her. I then asked the Stars for one more thing and when she looked up again she saw them perfectly shaped like a gigantic heart for her, shining bright, just like my love for her. I hoped she would understand the message.

'Oh look, the Stars love me!' she exclaimed, staring at them with big brown eyes which were now sparking in their reflection.

'Yes, they love you, everyone does,' I added hoping she would understand me but she only smiled back at me.

She then gently placed the star in the front pocket of her blue dress and I put her down to the ground thinking she could be tired now.

'Thank you so much Rupert, I will look after her and let her float from now on right above my hut, shining love upon me each night. You are truly an amazing...oak,' she said, hugging me with both arms, making me feel dizzy from the warm sensation of her body, and then she lifted the lantern from the ground, and quickly disappeared into the darkness.

'I am so happy to be a tree,' I thought to myself and then immediately, 'Did I just think that?'

Chapter 10

WRONG TREE

Stop throwing leaves at my face Robin!' exclaimed Rupert seeing a whirlpool of leaves dancing right in front of him.

'I am not throwing any leaves at you, you are losing them because it's Autumn,' replied Robin.

'What? Oh no, I am shedding leaves? I am going to be naked??'

'Yes. Completely quacking naked' replied Robin with a big crescent in his beak.

'Oh no, no, no, I cannot be naked, that's improper in front of a lady,' announced Rupert just before he had noticed Amara standing right in front of him. 'Amara, please help me!' he added in desperation.

'Ok, how about I knit a cover for you. You know, like from moss and stuff. Would you like that?' she offered.

'Yes, please,' he replied and a few moments later added, 'Ah, that's much better now. How do I look?' he asked, wrapped up now by Leticia and her squirrel friends.

'Oh, you look like...,' started Amara but Rupert interrupted her, ' Like what? How do I look? Tell me! Never mind, I am going to see for myself in the river,' he replied and as soon as he had looked into the glasslike water surface he stepped away as if he had seen a ghost.

'Amara, what have you done to me? You dressed me like an old grandma in floral curtains!' rumbled Rupert angrily.

'Sorry, we thought with Leticia that we would make a blanket which was a bit more colourful, you know with bluebells and roses. But I can see you don't like it, it's fine I will get those removed.'

'You know what, I am not feeling naked anymore and I am not cold, so thank you very much but I shall stay as I am, just as nature created me, I mean Forest Mother,' he replied taking the cover off, 'I will stay naked, otherwise other trees would laugh at me. They already are! Look at them over there. Ahhhrrr. And what about my nuts? Will I have no nuts now either? Oh no, I will be a nutless naked prince in a tree. It couldn't get any worse,' he whined.

'Don't exaggerate please, remember your acorns are your babies now...you have lots of them so I hope you can afford to support them,' replied Amara with a smile and a wink.

'Now that's not funny, hundreds of babies does not sound funny at all!' growled Rupert.

'No, you are right, I am sorry. It's not funny. It's hilarious!'

'And what about you? Will you have babies one day? I do hope I will, at least one when I am normal again. And I am sorry I cannot help you with that matter. It's not that I don't want to, it's just that I am... too woody for you,' he added.

'Ha! Yes, you are woody but I must say I like the look of some of your woody branches. However, let's just say I am happy as I am,' she replied and turned around, leaving Rupert alone with some time to reflect upon their conversation.

The next morning Rupert was slowly gliding along the riverside when he saw Amara hugging another oak. He was embracing her with his two branches.

'Oi, what's quacking happening here?' he asked, shocked by what he had seen.

'Rupert! That's you?' asked Amara, opening her eyes and gently releasing the oak.

'Yes, of course, it's me. Here. Not there Amara!' he exclaimed, getting angrier and added, 'Hey you, get your wood off my lady, will you?'

The other oak opened his branches and Amara stood there as if she had been caught cheating on her beloved tree.

'I'm sorry Rupert, I was very sleepy this morning, and having walked here I really thought it was you, he smelled of the same oakmoss and I just needed a morning hug. He didn't say anything so I assumed that it was..you... I am sorry,' she replied and ran up to him.

'Hey, nothing happened, we were just..' said the oak but Rupert didn't even let him finish the sentence and said; 'Hey you, Trupidoo, listen to me carefully now. If you ever do that again, you shall regret you were even born. Do you understand me?'

'My name is not Trupidoo and I tried to tell her...' replied the oak but Rupert would not listen and said; 'Let me make it clear to you. I would think twice before you pretend you are me again. Squirrels told me about someone you wouldn't want to meet in your worst nightmares.'

'Oh really? Who is that?' the oak asked with curiosity.

'His name is a nutcracker,' replied Rupert, 'so if you want to lose most of your nuts and turn into a wimp, keep doing what you are doing but I seriously wouldn't advise you to,' he added and hugged Amara with all his strength, making the other oak grunt and slowly move away without saying a word.

'I am sorry Rupi, I have missed you. I won't make that mistake again but if you changed your oakmoss fragrance into something more distinctive it would help,' said Amara with an apologetic voice.

Chapter 11

JINGLE NUTS

'It's freezing, arrrrgh,' whispered Rupert as soon as he had woken up on one frosty morning.

'It's winter,' replied Robin with a smile on his beak, giving him a big smooch on his huba which made Rupert cringe from the unexpected intimacy with him and the obvious statement to him.

'Yes, I know! No need to tell me that. I am naked after all,' replied Rupert.

'No, you are not naked, you have spikes on you.'

'Spikes? What spikes? I am freezing my nuts off here and you are making jokes. Not nice my friend.'

'You don't really have nuts anymore but you have frozen spikes on you. You know, icicles. Which I think makes you look quite sexy even though you seem quite stiff,' replied Robin with yet another smile but this time flying a bit further away from Rupert's branches in case he tried to whack him with them in anger.

'Ahhhrhrh, you drive me nuts sometimes!' exclaimed Rupert angrily, looking at himself covered in crystallised snow frost and icicles all over his tree body and added, 'Hey, just don't talk like this when Amara comes, that I look sexy naked and stiff, do you understand me?'

'Yes, boss, but I doubt she will fail to notice it. If you like, I can ask the badgers to knit a covering for you, would you like that?

'Oh ok, all I need is another granny plaid all over me. Amara and Leticia have already tried it once. No thanks, weirdo. I prefer to freeze my nuts off.. which I don't even have anymore! Ahhrrrr..'

'As you wish Rupi,' replied Robin and flew away knowing that talking to Rupert at his current emotional state could be a dangerous matter.

'There you are my darling,' said Amara approaching Rupert at twilight that day, 'How are you today?' she added with a warm smile getting closer to him and touching his frosty bark. 'Ouch, you are cold my dear. Almost frozen,' she added, 'It's winter!' she continued after a moment of hugging him tight as if wanting to warm his body.

'Oh my...yes I have noticed that!' replied Rupert clearly annoyed at yet another statement which was obvious to him.

'Look, I know you didn't like what I did before but this time I got you some covers that Mama Badger had made for you.' she said, and before Rupert even had a chance to object, sparrows surrounded his trunk with a checked plaid made from sheep wool.

'Ah, I knew it would be the right size. It fits you perfectly!' exclaimed Amara to her amusement.

'You mean, I look like I am in a woollen skirt?' replied Rupert looking down at himself, embarrassed but feeling a pleasant warmth from the soft wool surrounding him.

'Don't be silly, you don't look like you are wearing a skirt, and even if you did, so what? I still think you are sexy!' added Amara with a wink.

'Ok, well, anyway, I have prepared a surprise for you,' Rupert replied, trying to change the subject from this embarrassment.

'What kind of surprise?'

'Today is Christmas Eve so I decided to make all of this for you,' he replied and took Amara's hand leading her towards the passage through the trees into the meadow.

What was unveiled to Amara when they had emerged from the darkness of the surrounding trees was the most magical vision of her life. With every step on the squeaking snow, they were moving closer and closer to the twinkling lights among the frost-covered trees. When they walked into the tiny valley all the other trees around them were now twinkling with warm lights from winter fireflies, turning the forest into a light spectacle with frozen icicles reflecting sparkles in all directions. Snowflakes on the trees and ground turned the scene into a magical winter wonderland of pure whiteness surrounding them all over.

'Look, I have decorated a Christmas tree for you,' said Rupert, proudly pointing at a tall pine tree which was dressed with dried apples, sprinkled with holly, dried red berries, icicles, and dotted with snowflakes. Red squirrels were sitting all over it, wearing chains made with acorns hanging from their tiny necks. As soon as they had seen Amara approaching, they started moving their hips to the sides, wiggling their red tails and singing: 'Jingle nuts, jingle nuts...' and when amazed Amara looked at Rupert, she saw him holding a bunch of rats by their tails in both of his branches. They were smiling and showing off their tiny white teeth while squeaking and singing, '...jingle all the rats!'

'Do you like it?' asked Rupert shyly.

'Ohhhh, that's so sweet Rupi!' she exclaimed and her face lit up with joy and laughter, knowing that he put a lot of effort into this.

'Look what else I have prepared, it's not the end of the surprises' he added pointing at the bonfire with a wooden seat next to it and a small wooden table. It was illuminated by the warm light of candles dotted all around it and the whole area around the bonfire was surrounded by tall candles stuck into the ground, making the whole scene magical. Amara gasped from the most wonderful Christmas vision in her life.

'I know you love fireplaces and I am sorry I cannot give you a home with one. I wouldn't fit into the house anyway and you know that being a tree I should kind of stay away from the fire unless you would like to see me as... ashes,' he added giggling.

'Please stop it, Rupert, I love it, and this is more than I could ask for. It is, it is...magical' she gasped looking around with her eyes sparkling as if two fireflies had drowned in them.

'Here, take a seat my darling, I have arranged for the bees to make all these candles for you from beeswax, and here is a jug of warm honey for you to enjoy. They wanted to share it with you too,' he said when Amara sat down at the table, stunned by the effort Rupert went into to prepare it all for her.

'Thank you,' she whispered with gratitude for the most wonderful man-tree she had ever met.

'And here, I had an idea that we may bake some chestnuts in the fire. Would you like that?' he pointed at the chestnuts stuck into wooden sticks, something that the badgers had helped him to do due to his own clumsy branches.

'I would love that,' Amara replied and Rupert handed her the chestnuts on the stick, holding one such stick in the fire himself.

'Ouch!' he exclaimed a moment later, feeling hot flames on his branch.

'Careful, don't burn your pinkie finger,' she said smiling.

'Ha, ha, very funny, enjoy your chestnuts, I think I am going to pass, I am not a fan of warm nuts of that guy over there anyway. I have my own thank you very much,' he replied pointing at the tree smiling from a distance. 'But you, my darling, enjoy the warm nuts, you can even cover them in warm honey if you like!' he added.

'You lost your nuts in the autumn Rupert, remember?' said Robin flying towards him out of nowhere, 'Now that the squirrels have hidden them they don't remember where they have put them. I am afraid you are going to end up with quite a lot of children,' he added, shaking off the snowflakes that had just landed on his feathers.

'Ha, very funny Robin the Wood! I don't plan to have a lot of children.'

'This is the best Christmas ever!' exclaimed Amara eating chestnuts and gazing at the Moon peeking from behind the clouds, smiling at them.

'I am so happy you are enjoying it, I have made it all for you. When I am back to being a man I shall give you a proper Christmas at the castle with a ball and lots of jewellery as gifts. You will be the most gorgeous princess this kingdom has ever seen,' Rupert replied with nostalgia in his voice, also gazing at the Moon, 'But for now, I am grateful for this moment, the moment of seeing you next to me filled with joy and happiness.'

He then lifted her high up in the air and seated her on top of his crown. 'Thank you for being here with me,' he whispered, as she gazed at the sky filled with stars until the first snowflakes started falling on her face.

'Oh dear, I think it's going to be a snowy night. Don't worry, I have prepared a shelter for you if you would like to stay here with me. Would you like that?'

'Yes, I would, you know I would, I love being close to you,' she replied gazing into his big eyes just as he put her on the ground slowly starting to be covered in a fluffy white blanket.

'But before we do that, I have one more surprise for you. Close your eyes,' he said and she did exactly that.

'What is it? Please tell me.,' she begged but all she could feel was Rupert's right branch reaching out to her hand and leading her gently forward.

'Ok, open your eyes,' he said pointing at the frozen lake at the bottom of the hill they were standing on which was glistening in the moonlight.

'Are you trying to freeze me in a lake for later?' she chuckled.

'No...I have organised a slide for you to give you some Christmas fun. Would you like a snow ride down the hill?' he asked and before she had a chance to say anything he lay on the ground right at the edge of the hill swaying backwards and forwards with his crown at the back, lifted her up in the air and placed her gently as if on horseback right above his belly button that obviously was just an imaginary belly button now, 'I hope you are ready for this?' he exclaimed and pushed himself off the cliff towards the glistening darkness at the bottom of the hill.

'Ahhh, Rupert! I am sca...' screamed Amara, feeling flakes of snow hitting her face with full force and being scared of the fall she closed her eyes expecting the worst.

'Trust me my darling! You are safe with me! Enjoy the ride!' Rupert exclaimed with a loud laugh getting closer to the bottom and sliding right on top of the frozen lake surface.

'So? Did you like it?' he asked when they stopped in the middle of it.

'Am I alive?' whispered Amara slowly opening her eyes.

'Yes, you are, and perfectly safe, just as I promised. I would never let anything happen to you,' replied Rupert proudly, gently sliding on the thick ice from left to right.

Amara was watching the scenery of the most magical winter wonderland she had ever seen, with all the trees around them sparkling with the magic of fireflies. She kept gazing at the Moon slowly hiding behind the white clouds now, which sprinkled her warm (from excitement) cheeks with gentle snowflakes.

'Merry Christmas my dearest!' said Rupert winking at her when she had finally stood on the ice and he was holding her hand with his branch, sliding slowly to the shore.

'This was incredible Rupi, I really enjoyed it, can we do it again please?' she asked, exhilarated from the experience.

'Not now, maybe some other time, it would take me ages to climb up again. Let me show you to the place where you will sleep tonight,' he replied, leading her by the hand and not letting go.

'Here,' he finally said having walked up to a triangular structure that he had built close to another bonfire and lots of candles on the snowy ground, 'Look inside!' he added leading her inside and still holding her hand with his left branch, 'Come on, have a look inside!' he added with a warm smile.

Amara felt uncertain if she should enter the unusual structure made from hundreds of branches but seeing a warm light inside she bowed her head and entered it. It was the most romantic room she had ever been into. It was full of fluffy fur all over it which made her wonder where it came from but looking closely, she had noticed it was the foxes, hares and badgers gathered together into warm fluffy balls of cosiness, hiding their faces deep into their fur for a deep sleep but providing Amara with the warmth she needed on that winter night. In the middle of the room, there was a chandelier made up of candles. She looked back at the entrance and saw Rupert's smiling face peeking in.

'Do you like it?' he asked with a big smile on his huba.

'I love it but what about you, you shall be cold, all alone there without me.'

'Oh no, don't worry, I shall be right here and I will not be cold, I often get the bear to come and wrap his arms around me, falling asleep hugging my trunk really tight,' he added.

'Now that sounds a bit weird but if it makes you happy and warm...'

'Well, what else can a man do when he is a tree?' he laughed and closed the door with a wooden stick structure, wishing Amara a good night.

'I wish I could be with her now, cuddling her to sleep in my arms, feeling her beating heart next to mine. I so wish I was a man..and could make love to her in my warm arms...every night,' he thought and closed his eyes.

Chapter 12

RIVER TRIP

When Spring had come and my naked body was finally covered in fresh new leaves I couldn't be more excited about the new things I could do with Amara after the cold winter was now over.

'What other things could I do that I couldn't when I was a man?' I thought and immediately got a flash of inspiration of all the things I could do for Amara, now that I was a proper 'magic tree.'

'I could take her on a romantic boat ride down the river, it's just I don't think I could find a boat that would fit me, and nooo that would be a bit awkward,' I thought, and as soon as I did Amara showed up carrying a basket filled with freshly picked mushrooms which were glowing. I really hoped they were not magic mushrooms.

'Morning Rupi,' she said with a gleaming smile, making my heart melt instantly.

'Morning my beautiful! Did you sleep well last night? Protected by your shining little star?' I asked.

'Yes, I did, indeed. The star has been hanging happily above the cottage you gave it to me and I couldn't be more grateful and ecstatic that the Sky was so kind and let me have it. Thank you for this amazing gift once again. It is one of the most wonderful things any man has ever done for me. Until recently I was only faced with arrogant peacock men as if showing off their feathers to impress me with all the luxuries in the world, when all I ever really needed, as it turned out, was a Star from the Sky! she replied putting her basket on the grass by the river, 'And maybe magical Christmas with my prince in the tree..' she added.

'Here, since I can see that you like mushrooms, there is another one for you. Very pretty I say.' I handed her the lovely red mushroom with white dots that I had just noticed by the crooked oak in front of me.

'Rupi, do you want to kill me?' she asked, smiling.

'Me? No. Why? I want you to live forever just like me,' I replied and then realized what I had said sounded stupid because when I would go back to being a human I would only live for a short period of time compared to oaks.

'This mushroom is poisonous. It may look lovely but it's deadly to humans,' she replied confidently.

'Oh dear, I am so sorry, I shall look into getting to know more about this forest for you so that I don't make such a mistake again. Please forgive me,' I replied blushing, embarrassed that I did such a silly thing and almost killed my beloved. 'Anyway, I was wondering what we could do today. The weather is gorgeous, the sun is shining and I fancy a bit of an adventure. I was going to take you on a boat trip but where would I find a boat that would fit me??!' I chuckled, laughing at my own sense of humour in this strange situation.

'Well, I would love that actually but it's ok, I understand it would be a bit of a challenge for you. We can just stay here,' she replied with such a caring and understanding voice that I almost exploded from frustration that I couldn't do that for her.

'Wait, I have got an idea! I think we can do this! It will be fun, trust me and I think it will work!'

'What do you mean?' she said with visible surprise on her face.

'I will be the boat for you!'

'You will be the boat for me?' she replied with an even more astonished voice.

'Trust me,' I replied, and having moved closer to the river bank, I threw myself into its cold waters and shouted, 'Come on, jump on me, I can float with the current! I am a tree, remember?' and I reached my branch out to lift her from the ground and put her at the very front, making her the captain of my soul or...my trunk.

'You are crazy! But I love it! I have sat on you during the Christmas ride but I have never thought I would sit on wet wood like this and I looove it. As long as you don't shake me too much...' she exclaimed, just as we were slowly drifting away with the gentle current.

'I know I am but then, if I was a human, I couldn't do all that, so I better make the most out of it!' I exclaimed, surprised at so many of my own genius ideas.

'So where are you taking me?' Amara asked after a while.

'Well, where would you like to go, we can only go in one direction. This direction. Ha ha, with the current, so we would need to walk back if that's ok with you?' I asked a question that was a bit late to ask now that I was floating with the current, unable to stop.

'Yes, it's ok, I love adventures. Maybe we can stop at the badgers'? I heard that their babies were born,' she replied.

'Sure, I had better let you get off here, hold on,' I replied and lifted her by the waist and put her safely on the ground, before stopping myself from floating any further, holding onto the trunk of an old pine.

After I had climbed up to the solid ground soaking wet, I saw Amara giggling,

'What's so funny?' I asked.

'Nothing, you just look so incredibly...wet, a bit like a wet wolf!' she replied giggling even more.

'Thanks! Now I am not only a tree, I also look like a wet wolf! This day is only getting better!' I snorted and shook all the water off my leaves, sprinkling laughing Amara with a shower of water, and making her completely soaked in return.

'Look, now we both look like wet wolves!' I chuckled, watching her face turn serious and trying to squeeze the water out of her hair.

'I am glad that we both have the same sense of humour!' she replied not even showing a sign of anger at my little joke.

'Come on wet 'collie', let's go and see the babies!' I replied and put her back on one of my shoulder branches and smiled at her.

'I still like you, you crazy tree man!' she replied, holding tight to the branch as I moved swiftly on the ground, trying to make it less bumpy for her. It was a challenge indeed having to walk on tree roots, making me feel like a princess on heels.

'My dearest Rupert! How lovely to see you,' exclaimed mama badger as soon as we had approached her moss house.

'Look who I've brought! The most beautiful woman on Earth!' I replied and put Amara swiftly on the ground right in front of the amused Emily's face.

'This is Amara, my...my...friend' I stuttered as I suddenly didn't know how to introduce the woman I loved so much.

'Hi Amara, nice to meet you, my dear,' exclaimed Emily jumping up from excitement and rushing to hug her.

'I am so glad you finally have a girlfriend Rupi, it's about time you settled down!' she added, taking Amara's hand and walking her away from me.

'Girlfriend? No, we are just...' I replied but was stopped by Amara's voice, 'Come on my tree friend.'

'Me? She called me her..tree friend? Was I hearing right?' a thought went through my mind but seeing Amara's wink I knew she meant it or maybe...she was just jokingly teasing me.

'Oh, ok my girlfriend! I am coming!' I replied and followed them to the garden where Emily seated Amara on a tiny wooden log near the flower pot filled with lush lavender flowers in full bloom, making me feel dizzy from the sweet scent that had always put me to sleep.

'Wait here my dear, let me show you my precious treasures,' she said and rushed to the house.

'Treefriend? Like a boyfriend? Really?' I asked shyly, still not believing what I had heard but before Amara had a chance to reply I heard the strangest noise I had ever heard in my life,' 'QUUEEEEEE!'

'Here, there they are, my sweet little babies, this is Mikey and Tommie, my biggest sweethearts,' exclaimed Emily trying to be louder than the squeaking crying of her babies in the cradle which I had made for them with Robin.

'They are adorable, just beautiful' Amara replied, lifting Mikey or Tommie, God knows which one really because they both looked the same to me, and held him close to her chest, making him stop crying.

'Aww, they are such adorable gorgeous babies,' she said with a soft voice, making my heart melt again. I loved the way she was and everything about her.

'Come, Rupi, have a look look at.. Mikey,' Emily slowly finished her sentence.

I moved a bit closer and when I looked at Mikey's face, all I saw was lots of fur, a fat round nose, and tiny eyes that looked like two coin slots. It was the ugliest thing I had ever seen in my life. Apart from Robin when he was soaking wet in mud after he was thrown into it by his wife for not showing up at home till early morning.

'And... what do you think, Rupi? Do you want to hold him?' Amara asked, lifting Mikey high in the air.

'Oh, umpfpf he is so... lovely! But no, I don't think I am good with babies, you hold him' I replied moving away from that 'danger' slowly so as not to hurt her feelings.

'Come on, Rupert, you need to get some practice, after all soon you will also have babies, right?' asked Emily, almost throwing me off balance and ending up tripping backwards because I was unable to stop for a moment.

'Haaaa! Well, I don't think that's going to happen!' I chuckled knowing that in the current unfortunate state of affairs of me being a tree I definitely couldn't have babies with Amara.

'What do you mean, it will never happen? What if I want to have babies? What then?' Amara asked, making me move even further away till I bumped into the tree behind me.

'Hey fella, you are stepping on my roots!' I heard the voice behind me.

'Oh sorry, sorry, I didn't mean to,' I replied, confused about the whole situation.

'Well, when I go back to being a human I guess it will be possible then!' I replied trying not to commit to anything but giving her enough hope to leave this subject for now.

'And when are you going to be a human again?' asked Emily my most burning question that I also wanted to know the answer to.

'Ummm how should I know? As soon as I find that vicious Forest Mother, I guess. Robin is supposed to help me find her but he is busy right now with his missus and guess what! Making babies! Apparently, this is the mating season and his wife doesn't let him out of the nest for long, only to get more food supply and then he is forced to go back to work and make babies day and night. When you have such a desperate wife it can be very stressful, you know. Or at least that's what he told me last time he managed to get away from his mating sex prison, his home, to let me know he would be back to being my proper friend again soon.

'Ok, let's go,' said Amara, putting Mikey back into the cradle.

'Already? Why? You only just got here?' asked Emily, looking confused and putting the cradle back in the house.

'Why do you want to go? What's wrong? Is it because of what I said about babies?' I asked.

'No, it's just we were just stopping here for a visit, remember? You were supposed to take me somewhere,' she replied, winking at me again as if it had suddenly become a secret sign for us.

I winked back and said; 'Yes, indeed, we were going on a romantic adventure, we will see you soon,' I replied smiling at Emily and putting Amara back on my right shoulder branch.

'It was lovely to see you both! You are such an adorable couple!' she shouted just as we were moving away back into the forest.

'Oh thank goodness this visit has finally finished,' I thought.

Chapter 13

DRIFTING AWAY

'How about we stop here?' I asked floating on the river again towards the sunset with Amara relaxing on the top deck of the boat - me.

'Yes, it looks like a perfect place to stop at. That bluebell meadow with the view of the mountains,' she replied. I lifted her swiftly up again and put her on the riverbank, hoping I could stop holding onto the tree nearby but my wet branches slid across it and the strong current became faster, making it impossible for me to do so.

'Rupert, what's happening! Why are you not stopping?' I heard Amara's terrified voice.

'I can't stop, the current is too strong!' I shouted back, wondering what I was supposed to do now.

'Rupert, please stop, wait, let me help you!' I saw Amara running along the river, trying to catch up with me, and then I lost her out of sight.

'Here, hold onto this! I heard her voice again right above me, sitting on a branch and lowering it so that I could reach it.

'I..I...can't' I replied as the current speeded up even more, making it impossible for me to make any move and hearing a loud thumping sound, making me pray it was not what I feared the most.

'Hold on, it's a waterfall!' she screamed looking at me with a face full of fear and breathless from running after me.

'I..I..' I muttered, wanting to say I loved her just as it was clear to me that I would die now but I didn't have time to say it because I saw the edge of the merciless water, pushing me towards the end of my life as a tree.

I then fell down the waterfall.

I couldn't feel anything other than a loud thumping noise of water around me and the strongest power that I had no control over in my life. Then, I died. Or at least, that's what I had thought for a second, falling into the depths of the river with a big bang, splashing the water high up to the air and to the sides.

'Rupert!!!' I heard Amara's echoing voice underwater.

I opened my eyes, and... I was alive! Floating in a peaceful river again. With the remains of my strength, I grabbed the tree to the left and held it. I was safe. I had survived.

'Rupert...I am coming!' shouted Amara, seeing me smiling and getting out of the water slowly.

'Ok, my dear, take your time, I am ok,' I replied, coming out of the water and splashing it to the sides, 'I am ok, don't worry,' I added when she ran up to me.

'Are you ok? Are you hurt?'

'I am not hurt, just a bit tired. The current was too strong and I couldn't stop. I am sorry you had to experience this.'

'I was so worried about you, I thought I was going to lose you,' she replied, hugging me tight with both arms.

'I thought I wasn't going to make it and that I would never see you again either,' I replied and lifted myself, shaking off the water from my tired body, 'Here, I am ok, you see. All good,' I added but felt a bit dizzy and swayed to the side.

'No, you are exhausted, you need to rest, we will not go any further,' she replied, hugging me gently, helping me get my balance again.

'But we need to get back home. I promised you that we would be back in the evening.'

'No, we can't go back. It's too dangerous and it's getting dark anyway, you are too weak to walk up the river. We will stay here.'

'What? Are you sure you want to stay here? With me? But where are you going to sleep?'

'Well, I hoped that you would think of something...as you always do,' she replied, smiling at me and sitting down on a riverbank, putting her bare feet into the crystal clear water.

'Well, how about I make a bed for you?' I suggested and I put one side of my branches close together into a cradle and lifting some moss from the ground, I nested it for her.

'Tada!! There, it's your new bed. Do you like it? It will be high up enough to protect you from the wolves at night and if it rains at night I will make a little roof over your head so you will not get disturbed at all. What do you say?'

'You see, I knew you would think of something, you are incredible,' she replied and suddenly lifted her light blue dress and showing off her naked silhouette, she jumped into the river, making me dizzy from this unexpected vision.

'Am I dreaming?' I thought, not believing my luck in meeting the most beautiful creature on Earth. Amara was swimming as if she was born as a water nymph, or at least that's what I had heard about them from old tales. She splashed the water around her with the most incredible swirls and shapes, turning her swim into a magical performance. 'How could she do that?' I thought but before I said anything she exclaimed happily, 'See, now it's my turn to get wet!' laughing and diving under the water like a dolphin.

'Oh, I love my life and I love Amara,' I thought, and then 'Did I just think that? I am a tree! Still! When will I be myself again? And when will I be able to give Amara what she needs from a man?' I thought, worrying, but at the same time looking forward to our night together.

Standing there at dusk I started to wonder; 'What is love after all? Is it the touch of the skin of the beloved person? Is it the kiss that the person welcomes me with each day? Is it the look they give me when they see me walk through the door? Is it any of the physical sensations that I can experience as a human being? And how do I know if it's true? How do I know if it's honest and truly..love? There are so many questions in my head that need answering that I simply cannot sleep peacefully at night, not knowing the answer to them and not knowing what it truly means.'

Back in the castle, I have the perfect candidate for marriage that my father chose for me. She is beautiful, she can speak other languages and she can curtsy like a lady. Is that enough for me to love her and give her the respect and feeling she deserves as my wife and future queen? According to the king, she is the one for me. Our kingdom will be secure for as long as I am married to her, the Princess of the Eastern Kingdom but there is this constant annoying voice inside of me that keeps me awake at night. What if this isn't love? What if this superficial way of looking at marriage is not enough for me to lead a happy, fulfilled life? What if there is more for me to experience in this short lifespan? But then, I cannot choose for myself, My father has already done it and he has to be right. I have to trust him. Even though, I feel unsettled.

Now that I am a TREE I feel free. Free to choose what I want out of life and who I want to be with. I feel that Amara is the one and only woman for me. Even though she is just a normal girl and not a princess. But the biggest tragedy of all is that now...I am an ugly tree. I can't be with the Princess of the Eastern Kingdom and I can't be with Amara. I can't be loved by any of them. Who would love an ugly oak anyway? I can hardly walk if you can call this slow-motion sliding zigzag motion walking anyway. I can't give any of them what they need, a loving, caring man that I am, the magnificent prince, handsome and charming who can whisk them away to the sunset in a carriage. I simply cannot show my love to any of them, even though I only want to show it to Amara, the beautiful, innocent and caring girl, the most beautiful creature I have ever seen. I just wish, I wish she could know how I feel about her. And I wish I could tell her I am a prince after all. I mean I did but she only laughed, knowing I am just an oak, having a wishful thinking moment, joking and dreaming. How is this going to ever end? Why can't I just be normal and happy in love? What kind of love could I give her anyway in the state I am in? I can't cuddle her for goodnight in a warm bed, I can't kiss her every time I see her, I can't, I can't make love to her as a good man could. I can't, I can't, I can't... I am nothing and I feel nothing now I am a tree. There is nothing I could give her as a tree. I just want to... die. I want this pain and misery to end. I don't want to hurt her. I am not sure why she is so nice to me and talks to me about all our dreams..none of them will come true unless I become a human again. I hate that Forest Mother witch, it's all her fault. She did this to me. I want to find her and make her suffer just like she made me suffer so much. Unloved and unhappy, without the body I should be in now. How can I love without the body of a human being? Even though I can feel what I used to feel, I can't show it. How? Now? I feel it...I feel it so much it hurts but..it can't be real, can it? I can't show the warmth and compassion for the one and only true love of my life... Amara. I am a tree. Trees don't feel anything. This is horrible. But actually, I do feel...a lot and I feel...love. Ok, that's it. I need to find that Forest Mother. She is no queen of the Forest to me now. A horrible woman. Heartless. Cruel. But before I do, I am going to tell Amara..how I feel. Yes. I will tell her that I love her even though it's wrong and it's impossible for a tree to love a human, but I do so much that it hurts.

Chapter 14

LIGHTNING

When the darkness fell upon the forest in a moonless night Amara emerged from behind the ferns where she was drying from the evening swim and saw millions of fireflies surrounding Rupert and the dinner table that he had prepared for her.

The fireflies lit up in a gentle dance around Rupert and Amara sparkling as if the stars had descended upon the Earth, dancing in a synchronised way the Waltz of Love. After all, it was the mating dance that the males performed to attract females, hoping that the one shining brightest would get the best one. Amara's eyes filled with watery pearls, twinkling in the corners.

'This is for you,' said Rupert in a warm, caring voice.

'This is...this is...' stuttered Amara because she was unable to speak from being so touched by the gesture he had made.

Rupert was looking right into her eyes and he knew deep down in his core that she felt the same about him as he did. The whole world was swirling around them in the magical dance of love. Love that was all around them and love that was in their hearts. Love that penetrated every leaf, every stone, every gust of wind.

After what seemed like an eternity of looking into each other's eyes without saying a word Rupert whistled and fireflies gathered all around him, one next to another, perfectly surrounding every branch and every leaf. He looked as if he was on fire, emanating the most loving light in the middle of the dark forest.

'You see? And who is the brightest shining male in the forest tonight?' he asked with a wink and a cheeky smile knowing very well that she knew why male fireflies light up...

'You look..you look...' she started stuttering once again, 'You look divine!'

'I prepared all this for you. I did all this because...' now he stopped halfway through his sentence because he knew it was the most important moment of his lifetime, to confess his profound, deep and pure love to the most wonderful woman on Earth, 'It is because I love you,' he finally said and moved his eyes in the opposite direction, embarrassed by his confession whilst still being a tree and worrying what response he might get from the object of his affection.

'Rupert, I love you too,' he heard a gentle whisper and he felt as if he was being lifted in the air by the fireflies. 'I have always loved you. From the moment I set my eyes upon you by the waterfall I knew you were the one for me. I knew you were more than just a tree. I knew you were the most loving and caring spirit I had met in my life. I am sorry I was teasing you that I didn't believe you were a human in the tree. I knew all along and I knew we were meant to meet right there and then. We had been destined to be together forever.'

'Oh, Amara, thank you for your heart and thank you for your soul. I promise I shall look after you forever and ever. And as soon as I get back to being 'myself' again, I will give you the best life in the castle as my princess,' he replied lifting her gently high up in the air with his two branches and bringing her close to his chest, or where his chest would have been if he was a man.

Amara wrapped her arms around him and he could feel her pounding heart pulsating right through the whole surface of the bark, filling him with the most loving vibration he had ever experienced.

'I love you now and forever and I don't care if you ever get back to being a human. My love for you is like a rock. It is so solid that nothing would crush it, and if it did it would remain in the tiniest crushed piece. I don't care about living in the castle. I am the happiest here in this forest, with you. I shall never leave you and I will always care for you,' she whispered.

'Oh my love, I will love and protect you for as long as I live. And If I were to be stuck in this tree for five thousand years I shall love you for five thousand years. And when I die, I shall find you in the clouds of Heaven so we can be together in spirit for eternity,' confessed Rupert and squeezed her tiny body even closer to his bark.

'Ouch, Rupert, you are squeezing me too much. You are very strong you know,' she said looking up into his teary eyes and he released her to the ground.

'Look what I have prepared for you. Romantic dinner at fireflies' light,' he said proudly and as soon as he did, fireflies spread around forming chandelier-like structures hanging from the branches, just above the wooden table made of an old tree log and a stool made in the same way, only smaller.

Amara sat on the stool looking up at the stars twinkling in the darkness of the sky and the magnificent chandeliers.

'Look I prepared your favourite sauteed mushroom, wild berry juice, and fried acorns. And the mushrooms are not poisonous, trust me. Now I have gathered all the knowledge about them. I wish I could just ban the bad ones from the forest.

'Thank you so much. This is very kind of you. But I think the fried acorns would be more suitable for Olek and Leticia. I really would find it strange eating your nuts' she replied smiling.

'Yes, yes, you may be right. Well enjoy your dinner and I will just stand here and watch you. Luckily I don't need dinners to stay alive. All I know is that I can drink gallons of water through my roots, Olek said it may even be 50 gallons of water a day. Do you know how much that is? A ridiculous amount and when it comes to acorns. I guess it would be too weird to eat my own nuts or...babies too' he replied with a loud laugh.

'Yes, that would be very strange indeed. Don't you find it strange that you produce 'babies' even though you are a...' she replied but stopped, unsure how to finish.

'Yes I know, I know. When I found out that I would be able to produce acorns, which essentially are my babies because I as an oak have both female and male caskets, I almost freaked out. Olek and Robin had a great laugh rubbing it in my face a few times, asking when I was going to give birth to new babies. But I accept it now. I guess sometimes it's more useful to be two in one, more self-sufficient. And it's not like we could ever have babies, you and me anyway...' he added but stopped as he had just realised that if he stayed as he was, he could never have an offspring with Amara. 'That's why I am going to do everything I can to find Forest Mother and get her to remove that spell. It's really unfair what she has done. I didn't deserve it. Anyway, I have one more surprise for you tonight,' he added and pointed at the frogs coming out of the stream.

'Ummm, you want me to make friends with frogs now? Hopefully, you won't tell me to eat their legs...?' she asked, visibly amused by the sight.

'Nooo, well yes, if you like. But listen...,' he replied, and the five frogs, dressed in little bows made of reed, lined up on the rock right in front of them.

They were joined by a group of crickets who started playing their usual evening melody but this time with a twist because every few seconds the harmonised sounds of frogs croaking could be heard, creating a unified melody similar to 'Blue Danube' by Johann Strauss but not so accurate. Amara was watching the performance and smiling from ear to ear, gazing at Rupert's amused but proud face. She could not believe he had planned and organised all this for her in such a short space of time. 'What a man, what an oak. What an evening' she thought.

'Thank you very much guys, thank you thank you, you did a good job!' announced Rupert as soon as they stopped playing and the whole forest band quickly disappeared into where they came from.

Amara looked at his eyes and saw a wink. He then unfolded a wooden swing that fell from his left branch almost touching the ground. It was dressed in pink and white lilies on both sides.

'There my lady, would you like to swing with me?' he asked.

'Yes, I would love that! I love swinging!' she replied and sat right in the middle of the wooden seat. Rupert was gently swaying her backwards and forwards.

'Uhhhuuu more!' she exclaimed laughing, amused by this wonderful surprise.

'See, being a tree has its perks sometimes.'

'I am feeling a bit dizzy now. And sleepy,' she said after a while.

'Here, come and sleep in my arms, I mean the bed of leaves of my branches,' replied Rupert, and having lifted her gently with one branch he placed her in the comfort of the leafy bed cradle he had prepared for her.

'You will be safe here, right in my arms,' he replied and she soon fell into a blissful sleep hearing nothing but the crickets in the distance, continuing their night serenade.

Rupert was so happy he could have his love by his side. He felt complete. His eyelids were getting heavier and heavier but when he was woken by a loud bang he saw a powerful light across the sky.

'Oh no, the thunderstorm is coming,' he thought.

'What happened?' sleepy Amara asked, lifting her head up as she could sense something was wrong.

'Quick, I need to find a hiding place for you. You cannot sleep with me here. It's too dangerous,' he said, setting her down, looking confused, on the ground and moving away in the direction of the wall of rocks.

'Come, I need to find you a safe place to hide.'

'But I don't want to go anywhere without you, Rupert. Why can't I hide under your branches and stay close to you?'

'Because that would mean certain death to you. I cannot risk your life like this. The lightning is more likely to hit the tallest trees and oaks, which is me. I am a walking danger for you. I need to hide you in a cave,' he replied in a voice that was fading away in the strong gale moving all the trees around. The lightning struck again and again with a loud bang, the sky lit up with skeleton-like forms, making Amara more and more petrified walking next to Rupert who was now touching the sides of the mountain as if looking for an opening.

'Here, quick, get in there. You will be safe in this cave. I shall move away now because I don't want to stay too close to you,' he said, pushing Amara firmly into the opening in the rock.

'Don't worry, I shall come and get you as soon as the storm is over, ok my love?' he asked but she kept holding onto his branches as if it was to be the last time they were to see each other. Her eyes were filled with fear every time the burning light spread across the dark sky.

'I don't want to be here alone, please don't leave me. You said you would never leave me, and now you do. Why? Please stay close to me,' she begged with tears in her eyes.

'I am sorry. I have to do this for your own good. Please understand I am a walking death to you. And you cannot die, do you hear me? You cannot. I will not let it happen and he released his branches from her tight fists.

As he was moving away, the heavy drops of rain started to fall upon his leaves and when he was a few metres away powerful lighting struck him right through the middle, and for a split second, he felt a sharp pain as if he was going to burn and die. Amara saw it and, unable to stay in the cave, she ran towards him.

'Nooo! Rupert!! You cannot die!' she screamed running towards him but she heard no answer.

Then the silence and total darkness fell upon them.

Chapter 15

I AM DANGEROUS

'Rupert, are you ok?' whispered frightened Amara touching the bark, 'Rupert! Rupert! Please say something!' she exclaimed much louder this time.

'I am ok, I just feel like I have been hit..by lightning,' he replied and smiled as if it was actually funny.

'Thank goodness, I almost got a heart attack thinking that you...'

'That I what...'

'That you died.'

'And if I did, would you be sad?' he replied with a wink as if he was still considering it all a big joke.

'This is serious, why are you joking about it, yes I would be very sad and I am afraid I would die too.'

'What? Why would you die if I died? Don't even say that Amara, that's not funny.'

'So it's ok for you to joke about you dying but when I say it, it's inappropriate? Why don't you just get quiet now,' she replied, hugging him tight but he pushed her away and put her in the cave again. Standing close by he created a rain shelter right in front of its opening.

'See, I knew I had to put you in a safe place, I just knew what would happen.'

'How did you know?'

'I just knew. It is as if I had a premonition or something. I seem to know so much now that I am a tree, I never used to know so many things about the Universe and nature and animals, also about myself. I feel like I really got to know myself so much more, I feel I am part of this forest, part of everything and everyone, like I have become part of some collective consciousness. I feel that everything is interconnected in the Universe and even you and I seem to have this special bond which I have never felt before with any woman.'

'Yes, I know what you mean, I feel the same way too. If only more people felt the same. If only more humans understood more about our world which in fact is the same world but they see it from behind some invisible glass putting barriers between themselves and us.'

'You mean between themselves and us, nature. You are a human too so how come you understand as much as I do? You are not like everyone else or even me when I was a prince, a handsome one, remember?' Rupert replied with a grin.

'Yes, I do seem to know more because I have lived in this forest for so long and I took time to understand it. That's why I can talk to you,' Amara replied and hid a bit more into the cave because the rain was hitting the ground with a full force more and more and the bolts of lightning brightened up the sky, even though the loud bangs were heard far at a distance now.

'I am so happy I have met you, you are like a breath of fresh air and unlike any other woman I have met before.'

'I like the way you are too. You are unlike any other tree I have met before. You are crazy but funny and soooo caring. You are a true gentleman to me, just like a good man would be.'

'I am a man, remember? I am just stuck in this tree. Though not for long my love, I spoke to Robin yesterday and he said he knows where to find Forest Mother. As soon as I do, I will explain to her what happened and I will be normal again. I so want you to meet me in my normal self, not with these leaves and thick bark instead of my skin.'

'I am sure you are going to look amazing but I worry that when you do go back to your human form, you won't even look at me. You will go back to marrying a perfect princess for yourself and I will stay here forever, alone in the forest. You say you love me now but it may be different when you are a handsome prince again,' she replied with a hint of sadness and nostalgia in her voice.

'Umm, you think so? So you still don't know me. I may find it hard to express how I feel for you now in this form but I can assure you that there is no woman on Earth that I want more than you. You are the only woman for me. I love you so much,' he said and covered his eyes with one of his branches as if hiding the fact that he was blushing, even though it would be impossible to see it in the darkness and through heavy rain anyway.

'So you truly love me and want to be with me even when you become human again?' Oh, Rupert, this is the most beautiful thing I have ever heard in my whole life. See, I have been dreaming of finding true love and what I found was something more precious. From the moment I met you I have in fact been dreaming of finding true love with... you, my one and only soulmate for life. I feel you are the one I was meant to spend my life with..forever. I love you too Rupert!' she exclaimed and ran into his arms. He lifted her by the waist with his branches, and just as she tried to hug him and place a gentle kiss on his bark, he stopped and put her back on the ground.

'But I cannot promise you anything until I find Forest Mother and she takes away this spell from me, though. Go to sleep now,' he said and gently placed her in the cave, covering the entrance with sticks. 'I will come and get you in the morning. Sleep well. I will take you home in the morning,' he added and moved away, but he couldn't sleep all night, staring at the sky.

He realised that he and Amara simply could not be together for as long he was a tree. The lightning only made it clearer to him that he could not risk her life like this ever again. He began to wonder if he did the right thing confessing his love to her. Maybe it was a mistake. Maybe he should have waited till he became a man again.

'I want her to be happy with me but I may have to let her go. I may never find Forest Mother who will remove the spell and she deserves to find a good man who is a human being, a man who can look after her and love her in the best possible way. I cannot protect her like this. I shall tell her that it will not work. I want to tell her that I love her so much that I want her to be happy with another man...as crazy as it might seem. But this is the only solution to this madness of me being a tree. That's my biggest act of love to her. That's all I can do now. I need to let her go,' he thought and with a heavy heart watched the sun rising above the foggy valley, worried that the new day would not bring happiness to either of them.

Chapter 16

SACRIFICE

Amara enjoyed her breakfast consisting of freshly picked dew in a flower cup and a bowl of berries with honey that Rupert had left for her on the dinner table from the previous night. 'He must have been up really early,' she thought but she couldn't see him anywhere.

She was watching the remains of the fog lifting from the river and the sun rays piercing through the ferns as if the heavens had opened. She missed Rupert very much and she couldn't wait to see him again. She wanted to confess once more her deep unconditional love for him and gratitude for all that he had done for her. She had never felt more joyous and loved in her whole life. He protected her from dangerous animals, he saved her from the lightning, he took her on a river trip. There wasn't much he couldn't do. He showed her so much love and care that she wanted to finally tell him how much it meant to her. She pinned her hair into a flattering ponytail, put bluebells and Rupert's fallen oak leaves into it, and used some red berry juice to make her lips and cheeks beautifully seductive and glowing. She was ready to show him once more her pure love for him because he was the man, or a tree, that she had been looking for all her life. He was the best thing that had happened to her in the foreverness of the world.

When she took a few steps towards the river, clearly visible now that the fog had lifted, she looked around and saw Rupert standing alone by the river bank, as if sleeping. She approached him quietly, hoping he wouldn't hear her.

'You are up early. I have just been watching the sunrise, meditating, and thinking about you. Did you sleep well?' he asked before she even had a chance to touch him.

'Yes, I did thank you. How about you? Did anyone disturb you?'

'No, it was a pleasant and peaceful night. After the thunderstorm that is. I had never been charged with so much energy in one go. I could not sleep all night but it also gave me clarity.'

'I am happy to hear that. You see I came so early because…'

'Because you missed your handsome oak? I know, I know, not many of us are still around here. I don't blame you. I would rush to see me again in the morning too' he replied but quickly realised he had spoken quicker than he thought, knowing he probably sounded a bit arrogant but it was too late now.

'Yes, you are right, I have missed you,' she replied blushing, not really sure what to say next.

'Amara, there is something I need to tell you, my dear. Please listen to me. I know you love me…'

'Yes, I do love you very much,' she interrupted him.

'And I love you too but this isn't going to work,' he replied filled with fear, and moved his eyes to the other side of the river knowing what was about to follow. The most painful thing he would have to say in his life.

'You are a beautiful young woman and you need to find… a young, good man to take care of you. Look at me, I am just an oak.

There's nothing I can give you now. I could give you the world if I was a good-looking prince...but now? After last night I realised I would only put your life in danger and it's best if we stopped seeing each other. I want you to be happy and find true love. Not wasting your time with...me.'

'I see,' she replied in a hesitant voice, 'Well if that's what you think,' she added angrily as it was not what she had expected to hear.

'Yes. That's exactly how I feel. Look at me, I am an oak. And I really cannot give you what you need. You should just stay away from me. Once and for all,' he said in a firm voice and with a deep conviction that it was only for the best for both of them. I want you to find the love you deserve and I cannot keep you away from finding it, stuck with me here, deep in the middle of a forest.'

'But that night when you gave me the star from the sky you said that if I make a wish, it will make it come true. My wish was to live happily in love with you... You promised it would come true. You said you would always love me and that you will never leave me. And now you want me gone from your life forever? Why? It's not fair and it's not right! You are a liar! You never loved me. You never cared for me. You just played with my feelings pretending to be a true gentleman. You are a cruel, cruel man!!' she exclaimed, turning her back on him.

'Yes, I did say that I admit, but I cannot be held responsible for the wish you made. I didn't know you wished for our happily ever after' he replied and his voice broke, unable to continue with the conversation, trying to hold his tears from falling down his bark. Please understand, as soon as we get back home by the river it's best we stop seeing each other,' he replied firmly, hoping to cover the pain of losing the woman he loved.

'Ok. I shall do as you wish. You will never see me again. And I don't need you. I can be perfectly happy on my own as I used to be before you came to this forest and played with me like a fool. Like a fool. I hate you. I never want to see you again. Do you understand me? You are a horrible, nasty old...'

'Oh yes, say it! Say it!!'

'Old oak!' she exclaimed and turned away, swishing her long wavy hair in the air, as if it was a vision in slow motion, and ran away.

'Hey, wait! This is not the way back,' Rupert shouted back but she was already gone from his sight.

'She is gone. Forever. It's done. It's for the best. There's no other way. This was the right thing to do,' he started his internal monologue, 'I did the right thing. I had to do this. For her. Because I love her. I can't give her what she needs. I needed to let her go. Forever. It's all good,' he kept saying to himself, trying to convince himself that he did the right thing but in fact, the pain of his soul was so deep that he just wanted to melt with the ground and forget he ever existed...the pain of losing her forever was excruciating. He let her go so she could look for love with another man because he loved her, because he could not give her what she needed to be happy. 'I had to do this. I had to. Right, now I need to find that wicked woman who did this to me and tell her she achieved her goal. She punished me more than one might think is possible - by letting me find my true love when I am a tree... I need to find her and tell her I have learnt what true love really means. That it means letting the one you love go even if it means you are suffering. It means letting them follow their dreams even though you are not part of theirs. That the end of love sometimes means the biggest act of love one can give, that sacrificing yourself is the biggest act of love,' he thought and suddenly heard the thumping noise of trolls approaching fast. He knew what danger that meant for Amara. He spotted her walking back slowly towards him and he knew he had to rescue her.

Chapter 17

WEEPING WILLOW

'Quick,' Amara said and pulled Rupert's branch, helping him move in the same direction before he even had a chance to say anything.

'Wait, I will not run away from some nasty trolls. I shall fight them as a real knight would do.'

'Noo, if they realise you are actually a human in the tree they will cut you into pieces and make a huge bonfire from you. Trust me, there is no time to talk about it, just come with me,' she exclaimed and pulled Rupert's branch with an even stronger determination.

The thumping noise of the giant trolls getting closer made them shiver from fear. The swooshing sound of leaves and the cracking sound of broken branches was intensified by the vibration of the ground underneath each time the trolls put their giant feet down.

'Look, what's that?' asked Amara pointing at the open wooden door at the bottom of the humongous willow tree by the river, which was emanating an inviting beaming light.

'Hide in there my love, trust me I will be fine but you need to hide right now,' Rupert replied without hesitation.

'Noo, I will not go in there without you!' she exclaimed.

'You have to, just enter the door and hide in there. I shall stay here and pretend I am just a tree.'

'No, they will smell you, sense you are a human and kill you. I will not hide in there without you,' she replied with desperation in her voice.

'Amara, please, I will not fit through that door. You know that, don't you?' Rupert replied with a loving voice, but Amara got closer to the warm light which blinded her from within. When she moved even closer, she pulled Rupert's branch into it, holding it firmly in her hand and not letting go.

'Stop, let me go, don't make it more difficult, please,' said Rupert in a frantic voice, hardly audible now in the nightmarish noise of the trolls getting really close now, almost breathing down their necks.

Amara entered the light and looked back at Rupert. It seemed like an eternity as she stared at him with her begging and loving eyes. His sad wooden eyes told her to let him go but when she looked at the branch she was holding she saw it was... a hand. A human hand, holding hers tight, with strong fingers intertwined as if they were one. In that very second, she knew what she had to do. She pulled him even more and ran into the depths of the warm yellow light with all her strength. Holding Rupert's hand she ran and she ran, and she ran. The light was blinding her and she could not see anything other than hope in her heart. She closed her eyes and when she opened them again she was standing at the edge of a cliff overlooking the waterfall glistening in the sunset. The most colourful birds she had ever seen were flying above it and the sound of peaceful silence made her gasp from the vision.

'Look!' she exclaimed to Rupert without turning her head towards him. Her hand was still squeezing his so tightly that it started to hurt.

'So this is… this is what Heaven looks like,' he whispered and gently put his other hand on her shoulder. Amara looked at both of his hands and she knew that a miracle had happened. She knew that he was there, standing right behind her and if she turned around she would see HIM. Just as he truly was. A man.

'Rupert, you are, you are,' she stuttered when she had finally found the courage to look back at him, 'You are a human again,' she said finally, looking straight into his dark eyes but Rupert said nothing. He stared at her and then looked at his body because indeed he was a human being again now.

'I am free! The spell is gone! I am myself again!' he exclaimed and lifted Amara by her waist-high up in the air, turning around. 'Woohooo, we can finally be together now! I am Prince Rupert again! The evil Forest Mother lost! It is our love that made it happen!' he exclaimed, putting her down, squeezing her in a warm but firm embrace. Sparkles of light at sunset surrounded both of them in a loving aura of joy and happiness that they had never felt before.

'I am so happy! We can finally be happy now,' she replied and blushed at the sight of such a handsome man in front of her for the first time. His white shirt was glistening against his tanned skin and his wavy hair made him look like a model from a Forest Prince Catalogue.

'I have no idea where we are but this looks and feels like Heaven. I have never seen this part of the forest,' Rupert gasped gazing at the rainbow above the waterfall turning small fluffy clouds into colourful sugarcane balls.

'Me neither,' replied Amara, stunned by the surreal beauty of nature all around them.

'We will need to find a way to get back to the castle but because the sun is setting we need to find a safe spot to spend the night in. Look, there is a boat at the shore down there on a lake. Fancy a boat ride my lady?' he asked with gleaming teeth in an open smile.

'Yes, I would love that,' she replied, and holding Rupert's hand they strolled down the hill gazing into each other's eyes, unable to believe their new reality.

'So...what do you think? Am I what you had expected me to look like?' Rupert asked, looking at Amara in the hope of reassurance that he was good enough for her.

'Well, I was not expecting anything. I fell in love with you as an oak. I fell in love with your heart and soul. The rest didn't really matter and I never hoped for you to become this handsome man, knowing that there was little chance for that. But now that you are back in your body, I can say yes, I love the way you look. I love your dark hair moving in waves from left to right and right to left. I love your dark piercing eyes and your beaming joyful smile. I love your muscular body and that you are so tall. Yes, I love the way you look,' she replied with confidence, a huge relief for Rupert.

'I knew this nightmare of being a tree would not last forever. I just wonder where we are and why now? This really is a stunning part of the forest,' he added looking at the pink and blue butter-flies glowing at twilight right in front of his nose with one sitting down gently on Amara's chest, close to her beautiful bosom, so firm and shiny in the setting sun that he forgot about the whole world around him for a second.

The walk down the hill was a pleasant one and as soon as they had reached the white boat shaped like a swan with a long wooden neck at the end of it, they knew it was going to be their perfect night hideaway. The lake was the smallest and most picturesque location one could imagine, surrounded by tall trees and rocks wrapped in moss on one side.

'Come, let's spend the night on the boat, away from any danger before we set back to the castle in the morning. I want you to meet my father, the king, and my mother, the queen. I want everyone to see your beauty inside and out. They shall love you as much as I love you. You will be my princess forever.'

'Wait,' Amara said with hesitation before following Rupert into the boat, 'What if they don't like me? I am no princess, I have no dowry, I have no title or a castle. I am just Amara from the forest and I love nature, animals, and this beautiful world. I haven't got anything apart from my love for it all and you. But is it enough? Is my love for you enough for your family to accept me? Will they?' she added in a worrying voice.

'My love,' whispered Rupert, 'of course, they will absolutely adore you. They will be happy for my return and for my happiness. We shall have the greatest wedding this land has ever seen. It will be the day to be remembered forever. Trust me, my love, just follow me now, just like I have trusted you following you through that door to this Heaven,' he said, taking both of her hands and pulling her gently to the boat which was upholstered with soft moss, sweet-smelling jasmine flowers, pink rose petals, and white lilies, making Amara feel dizzy from this sweetest scent on Earth.

The boat was now surrounded by a herd of majestic swans which came out of nowhere and bowed their long necks for Prince Rupert and soon-to-be Princess Amara.

'Sit down, let me take care of you now,' Rupert said and started rowing the boat towards the centre of the lake which was calm like a glass surface and the swans escorted them as if leading them to Heaven.

There was not even the slightest movement in the air and the sky was slowly turning into the darkest colour of blue. The twinkling stars were lit up one after another as if the Star Guardian was turning them on one by one. The sun was now almost gone behind the mountains. Amara was piercing him with her warm, loving eyes filled with an admiration for his strength, kindness, and love for all that surrounded them right now. She knew Rupert fell in love with this forest as much as she did and for the first time, she felt a slight feeling of sadness. Sadness that they would leave it to live in a world where humans live by their own rules. Where humans do not always show respect and regard to the beauty of this world. Where money, power, and position are what matter the most. Where materialism is on a pedestal and where feeling at one with the Universe is considered stupid, childish, or witchcraft. She loved Rupert with all her being and she knew he was her soulmate but at the same time she knew by choosing to love him, she had to sacrifice all of this. She had just realised that love was a choice, and often a sacrifice. It meant choosing one path over another. She knew well that things could not be as they were until now, and in that very moment, looking at Rupert's sparkling eyes she almost wished he was still a gorgeous oakmoss smelling tree.

'What are you thinking about?' Rupert interrupted her internal monologue as if he had suspected something wasn't right, 'You seem to be very dreamy. Is it about me? I love the way you look at me. I am so happy,' he added, stopping the boat right in the very middle of this jewel of a lake.

'I was just appreciating this moment. Tomorrow we will be far from here and I want to remember this forever,' Amara replied, just as she was being lifted up to stand close to Rupert's chest.

He was so close she could sense his beating heart and his fast breath from rowing was so comforting she forgot about the silly thoughts she had just had. She was the happiest she had ever been in her whole life. She lost herself in the intoxicating smell of his skin, smelling of fresh dew and woody tones as if he was still...an oak, and when she closed her eyes for a second she imagined that... he still was.

'I love you with all my heart and soul. I want to make you happy for the rest of my life. I am now grateful to Forest Mother who had imprisoned me in this forest and, as much as I hate to say it, turned me into an oak. Without it I would have never met you. I would have led a life filled with superficiality, snobbism, lies and falseness, lavish parties with no meaning because my search for love was always meant to be here, with you. You are the woman of my dreams and standing here now under the sky filled with millions of stars as my witnesses, I now pronounce I am yours, forever and more. I shall worship and cherish your existence by my side. I shall never leave you, I shall never betray you, I shall never hurt you intentionally. I admit, being just a man I may make mistakes and I will make you angry not once but maybe even twice. But if I do, please tell me how I had wronged you and I shall do all in my power to correct my behaviour and make sure I never do that again. I shall be the mature, loving, and caring man you deserve to have. I shall be the best version of myself thanks to you,' he continued when he was gazing deeply into Amara's eyes, reflecting millions of stars shining above them.

'And I shall do that and more Rupert. I shall love and cherish you as my man, as my best friend whom I shall make angry sometimes too. So please forgive me for my imperfection as a human being in advance, as this is only part of our human existence. I shall do all in my power to show you my love, forever and more. I shall speak to you in my dreams and ask you for forgiveness at each sunset. I shall communicate with you with and without words. Wherever you are in the world, I shall send you rays of loving energy, radiating from the depths of my heart so that you always feel I am with you, by your side, loving and caring for you. You may go to war, you may go to explore foreign lands but be assured that my heart will always be connected to yours. And when you wake up in the morning you will know each day that you are not alone. I am with you. Because when I wake up in the morning I shall say: Good morning my love, my heart, my soulmate. Forever and more,' replied Amara.

This moment of confessing profound love to each other was sealed by the gentlest and most loving kiss they had both imagined. Rupert took Amara's face in the palms of his hands and holding her head gently he placed his warm, wet lips upon hers. The union was finally made in spirit and in flesh. The two souls pure and filled with love were as sacred as the sky above them. It was the most passionate kiss this forest had seen. They drowned in the sweet foreverness of their passion and their existence. Right there and right now nothing else mattered. Nothing else could have stopped them from living their lives to the fullest. Nothing was able to destroy the joy, peace, and passion that they had finally found.

'You are mine now. In the eyes of this Forest and the Sky, the Stars and the ever-present Wind I have made you mine. And I am all yours,' said Rupert and went down on his knee whilst still holding Amara's both hands because the boat made his move a bit wobbly.

'I haven't got a ring for you right now but I would like to promise you that you shall receive the most beautiful ring with huge rubies, emeralds, and diamonds that I can find for you in the whole kingdom. You will be showered with the most precious jewels, we shall dance to the Waltz at parties just for us and make love in damask cotton bed sheets, enjoying every single day and night for the rest of our lives. Right now I just want to ask you; Will you do me the honour of becoming my wife?'

'Yes, of course, yes!' Amara exclaimed with a smile and Rupert lifted himself up from the knee and kissed her passionately, making the boat sway side to side, in the magical moment of a union of two souls in the middle of the lake, in the depths of the magical Deer Wonderland Kingdom.

He then took a tiny lily and wrapped its stalk around Amara's ring finger. Its white petals were shining with sparkling dew in the light of the Moon and stars.

'It's the most beautiful ring you could have given me!' she exclaimed from joy and hugged him tightly, feeling his beating heart in her own chest and the touch of his warm skin made her feel dizzy from the still unexpected feeling of his human body, which was different to the feeling of the rough bark of his trunk.

The darkness was getting deeper and deeper but thanks to the hordes of fireflies dancing around them, reflecting their pulsating dots of light, and stars shining brightly in the sky, it was the most magical setting for Rupert and Amara to finally unite in mind, body, and spirit.

'I love you,' whispered Rupert in her ear and she felt like fainting from the sensation of the most wonderful blissful feeling she had ever experienced. He placed his strong palms at her back, holding her tight.

'Rupert, please, I can't breathe!' she whispered smiling, feeling his passion for her with every molecule of his body as if he hadn't had a body for a long time and he was desperate to feel it. And hers.

He kissed her behind her left ear, inhaling the sweet intoxicating scent of jasmine flowers in her hair which she always wore, and lavender that she carried in her dress pockets.

'You smell like Heaven,' he whispered, kissing her gently behind her ear, giving her shivers over and over again. He then slowly unwrapped her from the leather straps of her corset and gently pulled her dress off her, leaving her body naked in front of him, just as the perfection that she was created.

'You are so beautiful,' he whispered into her right ear, running his warm thick masculine fingers all over her bare back as if he was playing the violin like the most skilled virtuoso.

Amara was gazing at the starry sky, loving the sensation all over her body, wrapping her arms around his strong muscular back, something that was a totally different experience to touching his moss-covered thick bark as an oak. Rupert then gently turned her around so she was facing the Moon illuminating her naked body and she was now feeling his naked body behind her. He was moving his fingers up and down her belly, her arms, thighs, and firm breasts. He squeezed her smooth skin with his strong arms over and over again, making her gasp for mercy every time he did. He then released it and made her beg for more of the flesh sensation that she had never experienced before. He kissed her neck after moving her silky smooth hair to one side, gently, with his lips and then with his tongue, clasping his lips as if he wanted to suck her all in, making her freeze under his spell, the spell of the most incredible physical passion a human can experience. He then touched her breasts, squeezing them tight and then letting go, circulating his fingers all around the most sensitive parts, making her gasp for more, breathing more and more loudly. She was touching his hair with her arms reaching out behind her. One of his hands stayed on her firm breast and another slid down below her belly button to the area which she didn't know existed before. His gentle movements with his fingertips almost made her lose consciousness, feeling as if the life she had lived so far was a lie, not knowing what real life was all about; experiencing this Heaven on Earth in this magic part of the forest. Rupert then turned her around again and kissed her passionately on the lips, making her breathless once more. She looked up at the stars once more but she realised she didn't have to. With her eyes closed, she could see all the stars of the Universe swirling all around her, with her back being wrapped in the most passionate and strong embrace of the man she loved so much.

'I love you so much,' she whispered back when he finally released her lips from his.

He looked at her lovingly in the sparkle of the moonlight and kissed her forehead. He then lay her body on the warm soft moss-covered lilies and gasped when they united as one and only soul that was once lost. Amara couldn't believe what was happening to her. She felt as if she had returned home. As if she had always been homeless until she found peace in his arms. She knew he was the part of her soul that was always missing. She knew he was her Twin Flame. Rupert kissed her lips, her neck and squeezed her tightly as if they truly were One. He moved his hips faster and faster, making her gasp for air from under his strong arms. She was inhaling the remains of his woody oakmoss scent that she loved so much. She felt the ecstasy that no words could ever describe, that nobody could truly understand. He then pulled her hair so much that it almost hurt but she didn't mind because she felt she was his. Now and forever, no matter what, no matter what anyone might think, she knew it was the end, and the beginning. He then stopped moving on top of her and hugged her even more, she could feel his wet skin on her cheeks. They were both experiencing bliss. As if they belonged to each other from the very beginning of the Universe, as if they had finally returned home. To each other's warm arms. The passion they experienced was out of this world and they knew they belonged to each other forever now.

They then lay down to sleep, gazing at this magical night performance and hearing nothing but the crickets and frogs singing their serenade. Amara's head was resting nestled into the left shoulder of Rupert's chest, who kept kissing her forehead gently to comfort her and show her how much he loved her. Their eternity together had been decided. Right there...on that boat, in the light of the Moon and millions of stars.

'From now on I will always look after you. I will protect you from evil and cherish you in moments of joy. Our new life is only just the beginning now,' he whispered with passion but hearing a deep and calm breath of Amara he knew that she must have now fallen into a sweet dream.

He closed his eyes and drifted off into sweet dreams as a human again.

Chapter 18

TRUTH

The morning fog had lifted just above the lake surface when Rupert opened his eyes. The sun cast warm sun rays on his cheeks and illuminated the lake in the colours of orange, yellow, and sparkling gold.

'Morning my love,' he whispered, having noticed that Amara's head was still in the exact same position as she had rested it the night before and it seemed as if she had not moved all night.

He touched her hand which was slightly cold and pale at dusk. A cold chill went down his spine and he lifted himself up, resting Amara's head on the moss. She seemed to be in a deep sleep but she did not make the slightest move. He touched her porcelain cheeks and whispered; 'Amara, wake up! It's morning now. We need to go to the castle now,' but her faint breath was so shallow that for a moment he thought she had died.

'Amara, my love, please wake up, please..wake up!!' he screamed in despair now but she did not move.

In a sense of panic, he moved to the boat seat and started rowing frantically towards the shore. Gazing at the lifeless body of his beloved woman his eyes swelled up in tears.

When he had moored the boat he lifted Amara into his arms and carried her to a sunny spot on the meadow.

'What's wrong my love? Please talk to me! How can I help you? Are you ill? Please say something Amara, you cannot just leave me like this,' he exclaimed in an even more desperate voice which was now heard even across the lake.

He put his sweaty from stress forehead close to her chest and listened to the faint beating of her heart. It was slow and hardly audible. He was relieved that she was alive but he could not understand what had happened to her.

'It is because of you, Rupert. It is only because of you,' he heard a familiar voice coming from the ferns as if emerging from Hell itself.

He looked up in its direction expecting to see someone but to his surprise, he saw Robin sitting on a branch just above him. He was glad to realise he hadn't gone mad hearing voices.

'Robin! It's you! How did you get here?' he muttered his first question.

'I followed you both through the magic door. I was curious where it was leading. Hope you don't mind?'

'No, not at all,' replied Rupert, happy in a way that there was someone else he knew in this beautiful but now scary place where Amara was ill, 'But why did you say it's because of me? What's because of me?'

'Amara, she is faint and weak because you have turned into a man now. I know it's not something you wanted to hear or would have expected but that's the truth, my friend.'

'What do you mean because I am a man? What has that got to do with her? It was me who was under the spell which thankfully does not work anymore and we can be finally happy. I am taking her to the castle today so we can get married.'

'If you do that, she shall die. She cannot live much longer without you because...'

'Yes, I know she cannot live without me because I love her...'

'No, because you are not a tree anymore!' exclaimed Robin because Rupert simply did not let him finish a sentence.

'She cannot live because I am not a tree anymore? What on Earth are you talking about? Please tell me it is some sick joke that both of you had arranged to torture me a bit longer,' he replied standing up tall now and pulling a dangerous looking face. His heart was beating fast expecting to hear the worst but hoping for the best.

'She cannot live when you are a man because she is your... dryad and you were her oak. She is not a human as you had thought. At least, that's what I have heard from the squirrels down the valley. I didn't believe them when they first said it and I didn't want to worry you but I can see that unfortunately, they were speaking the truth. By choosing to be a man, here in this magical part of the forest you sentence Amara to death. She can only live and survive thanks to you being a tree. As a dryad she belongs to you, she lives thanks to your energy because essentially she is part of you.'

Rupert closed his eyes whilst he was listening to Robin's confession which seemed like a death sentence to both him and Amara. He knew what that had meant. He knew what this would mean for both of them. He knew he could not let that happen because he couldn't let the woman he loved die. He knew he had to make a choice. Either she lived and he died as a man or he lived as a man but stayed forever grieved over the loss of his beloved woman.

'In that case, I must take Amara back through the magic door in the weeping willow to the other side of the forest where I shall be a tree again and she can live. Yes, I must do this now. There is no time to waste. I cannot let her die,' he said and got down on one knee to put his arms around the faint body of his beloved woman, lifting her up.

Amara's head was now dangling lifelessly as he was carrying her up the hill and towards the tree door. He didn't even care or notice if Robin was following him. All he knew was that he had to let her live. That's what love was all about. To love is to let live. Love had no other choice. There just could not be another choice of true love. He then entered the magic door emanating with beaming light knowing that there was no going back now. That he had to go back to being an oak forever because he loved her. He had to do it.

For her.

For him.

For them.

He also knew he had to find Forest Mother now, no matter what.

Chapter 19

TO LOVE IS TO LET LIVE

When Rupert opened his eyes he saw Amara standing next to him and smiling lovingly.

She was fine. She was healthy. She was alive. It worked. They were back in Deer Wonderland Kingdom and he was once again an oak.

'How are you?' he asked with love and care in his voice.

'I feel like I've had the strangest dream, that you were a man and we were on a boat and we..' she replied slowly and started to blush.

'Now that sounds like a dream come true. Shame it wasn't real,' he replied, knowing she must have just lost touch with reality because of what had happened but he couldn't tell her the truth about it all.

He just could not. His words stuck at the back of his throat. He knew she could not know about the fact that she was a dryad and that she would die if he stayed a man. He knew that she would not let him sacrifice his life for her.

'When you gaze at the dark clouds sliding across the sky at twilight and only a few rays of dark yellow and orange light come out from the horizon at sunset you must know that you are not alone. You must also know that you are not the one who created it all and you know you are not the one who controls it. You must know that there is a more powerful force than you. You cannot stop the rain, you cannot start the sunrise. Only the secret power of the Universe can... but how? How can it be done? With such precision, with such predictability? After each night, another day always comes. How come it never fails, and it is never late? Who stands behind this magnificent show created especially for us, simple humans and trees to experience it for as long as we live, to see and to appreciate it. But do we? Do we appreciate this beauty that surrounds us? Or do we choose to ignore it? Now that I am a tree it feels comforting to know that there is a powerful force of the Universe because that means that power may be listening to me. It may be listening to my thoughts, desires and maybe, just maybe it will respond to it. Not like a genie in a bottle but more like a loving and caring force that is here to help and support me and you in this physical journey of the soul. I find it comforting to know I am more than just this physical body... currently of a tree, normally of a prince. I find it empowering and I would have never changed it for any other experience in the world... to find out, to discover who I truly am. A soul, energy interconnected with everything and everyone in this world, a creative mind that can desire, hope, dream, and experience..love. But there is so much to learn and experience, so much to learn, so much is needed for my growth. I feel as if I had lived before in a different world, in different times, with different lessons. I feel now that I have been on this journey for a long time, eager to learn about who I am for much longer than my current age indicates. I feel I have been on a soul journey to salvation and I was meant to learn my final lesson, of what LOVE truly was. It is not the beautiful eyes of a maiden, it is not the sleek hair of a woman, it is not the flirtatious smile of a Princess of the Foreign Kingdom. It is sooo much more. It is the feeling in the very core of the soul of the one standing in front of me, stripped bare from titles, material status, physical beauty, even though beauty is not lacking here in your case. True love is seeing but not through the eyes. True love is seeing through the soul, the very core of my being, my everything. When I am in your presence I feel all that you are, all that you have been, and all that you can be. I feel YOU. The most beautiful soul I have ever met.

The most imperfect soul I have ever met.

The most perfect soul for me.

I just hope, I just hope, that you can feel the same about me. That you can see me with the eyes of your soul. I don't have a body. I don't have a stallion to ride on. Not anymore. I don't have a castle to live in. Not anymore. I am just like you. A soul seeking to connect with another soul. You.

And I choose you because I love you.

Because you are the one I love.

Because you ARE love to me.

When I think of love, I think of..YOU.

You and I are two flames burning with so much desire to share our love we could light all the stars of the dark sky for centuries.

Together we can explode with so much loving energy, the world would change overnight.

Together we can change the world by first changing the way we are.

Together is our power.

Together is our mission.

We can love, dream, hope, and exist as individuals.

But why would we?

When together we can illuminate the world with Everlasting Love.

Together is our destiny.

Only together.'

Rupert finished his monologue of what true love really meant to him, describing it in words, even though words are not the most perfect way to describe something that is already perfect. Looking at Amara now he suddenly felt embarrassed about his emotional confession but she only looked at him and said smiling;

'I see you in the same way you see me. I see your soul. I feel your heart and I feel your love. I love that you always care about my safety. I love that you always care about my well-being. I love that you always care about my happiness. You are the most loving and caring man I have ever met. You are the man, or actually... an oak I have been searching for all my life. But you need to accept who you are and love who you are before it can truly work. You cannot reject me every time you feel insecure or unhappy in your own skin or... bark. You are who you are and you have to accept it..now or it will never work. I cannot love but at the same time feel rejected by you. This is not safety, this is not bliss. It is a constant worry that one day you will just tell me to go to hell because you have a bad day about being a tree. You have got to get over it and it will be fine, trust me. Forest Mother will not help you. Nobody will help you with this matter. I feel you will stay as you are, a handsome tree, forever but will you accept it and be happy living with me in the forest? Can you do that Rupert?'

'Noooo you ARE WRONG... I WILL FIND Forest Mother and she will take the spell away and turn me back into a human again so that we can be happy. I promise you this is the only way WE can be happy together, this is the only way I can make you truly happy with no compromise, no sacrifices. But I don't want you to sacrifice your whole life for me. You deserve to be with the most loving and caring man in the world. Me, of course, but in the body of a human. Not like this, not like now. This is wrong... I am sorry Amara but maybe you deserve someone better. I will never accept who I am now. I will never be who you want me to be. I want to be myself again. Only then I can be the ONE for you. Only then I can give you the love you DESERVE. But because we know it may never happen, I think it's best you found a REAL man, not a bloody oak. I think it's time I let you go...forever. I think it's finally over between us now. You know it and I know it. It can never work. It can never happen. You deserve a warm, safe home and you deserve to be loved like a woman can be loved, with passion and ecstasy, and all I can do is scratch your soft skin with my branches when I hug you. I feel devastated that I cannot be the man for you. I need to let you go but trust me when I say I will be back. I will be who I am meant to be and come back to get you. I will put the wrongs to right. I will find a way. For me. For us. There must be another way. But for now, goodbye my love.'

'Nooo, please don't leave me! Forest Mother does not exist, it's just your fantasy. I have never seen her, she will not help you, she will not rescue you. If you go and leave me now I shall go my way but I will never forgive you for leaving me like this. This is cruel and egotistical. You are doing it for your own pleasure and ego but not for me. Stop saying it is for me and for my good. It has nothing to do with me. I told you I love and accept who you are now but you never ever listen, you know better so off you go but NEVER come back to me as I will have no mercy upon YOU. I will not forgive and forget. I will not love you AGAIN. Love is not a game. Love is what is NOW. But right now all there exists is sadness and disappointment. I see that will never be good enough for you, I will never be perfect enough for you, will I? You think you need to CHANGE FOR ME TO LOVE YOU.

Well, you are wrong.

But wrong you shall stay forever.'

Chapter 20

TREE MASTERS

Finding Forest Mother was not as difficult as I had thought.

I didn't actually find her.

Staring at the top of the hills I noticed a figure of a woman wearing a long green gown sparkling like gold in the sunrise. I blinked my eyes just to be sure I was seeing it for real and there she was, a blond-haired beauty, standing on the hill. I knew it was Her. I knew she was the woman who did this to me. I simply knew she was the Forest Mother that I had to speak to. Suddenly the blinding light set upon her. All I could see was the stream of light beaming from her as if the Sun had just descended upon the Earth. I had no idea what it all meant but I had a feeling she had special powers. Seeing her filled me with an overwhelming and beautiful feeling but at the same time...I felt scared.

'Robin, I need to speak to that woman! Look, that's Forest Mother! I need to speak to her. Are you coming with me? I need to get to her as soon as possible,' I said as soon as he had landed onto one of my roots sticking out from the ground.

'Oh, I don't think it's a good idea,' he muttered mysteriously.

'Why? She is the one who did this to me. I need to find her and tell her to take the spell off me and Amara. She is the one who did this to us, I am sure. She must live behind those hills, see!?' I replied, pointing with my branch at the peaks of the hills glistening in the setting sun.

'I am sorry to say but I doubt you will ever make it there. The hills are a border between the Deer Wonderland Kingdom and the Kingdom of Trepolis, the so-called Tree Masters. Their necks are made of tree trunks and their long hair is in fact made of hundreds of little leaves growing on thin branches. They are fierce, they use trees as their warrior army and they don't let anyone pass through their land just because they want it, like you. Ever since they had forced the humans out 2000 years ago, they built a tall wall made of thorn bushes around their kingdom to protect it. No outsiders are ever welcome. Nobody really knows what caused such a fierce reaction but one thing is sure. They hate humans and they hate everyone who isn't part of their tribe. A few lost souls who had dared to enter their land were captured, quartered into pieces and their remains were put on display for others to see on top of that hill. She may be Forest Mother but they say she is the Guardian of all the land, good or bad and she is invincible. She lets everyone lead their lives according to their rules. Like in this forest, you cannot kill deer or you will be punished.'

'Ok, ok I get it. I like that story. But you are a chicken.'

'I am no chicken, excuse me!?'

'But there is one upside to this,' said Rupert smiling with his huba from the left branch to the right branch.

'And what's that?' asked Robin with curiosity in his voice.

'I am not a human,' replied Rupert, chuckling from mad laughter because for once his tree existence was about to be useful. 'But

I do understand my friend, that you are too scared to go with me. No problem. I do need to get to her no matter what, even if it means risking my life as a tree or a human. This nightmare has to end. Also, I'm not sure if you remember but you are not a human either. So... are you coming with me or not Robin the Wood as all the squirrels call you?' asked Rupert with a giggle of a madman or simply a mad oak.

'I.., I,' replied Robin but before he was even able to finish, Rupert pulled his roots from the ground and started walking away from him. 'Oh quack, I'll go with you. Tree or not, you won't survive without me! I will quacking protect you, don't worry my friend. Bffs forever, remember?' he shouted, flying next to Rupert. 'My missus will kill me anyway, so I'm not sure what is better. To die in the evil forest or from my wife's frying pan for not telling her where I've been so long,' he thought but quickly put this worrying thought behind him and jumped on Rupert's tallest branch like a captain of the ship, navigating through the forest into the darkest of darkest places on Earth. 'By the way, why do the quacking squirrels call me Robin the Wood?' he asked.

'Oh, dear I think the whole forest knows why, especially your wife,' replied Rupert with a wink, making Robin blush for a long time.

Entering the Kingdom of Trepolis ruled by the Tree Masters was pretty obvious and did not require any specific signs since the signs were already there. The forest turned into gloomy and misty darkness filled with thick fog. The birds stopped singing. It was so quiet that all they could hear was the swishing of Rupert's leaves.

'Robin, are you ok?' Rupert finally asked, trying to break the awkward silence.

'I am for now, not sure how long for,' he muttered, and as soon as he had said that, a giant spider came out of nowhere, staring at them with its red shining eyes which were as big as two bread loaves.

'Oh! Here we go, we have company,' said Rupert and in that very same moment, the spider jumped on his face and he could hardly breathe.

'Oh quack, get him off!!' he heard Robin screaming above his head but the vile creature just squeezed its arms and legs around Rupert and he knew he was in trouble.

Rupert inhaled the biggest breath possible and blew the air through his huba as if the tornado had opened its evil eye and there it was, the spider hit the opposite tree and fell lifeless on the ground.

'Oh yess! You quacking killed him Rupert! You are so brave! I knew I could trust you!' exclaimed Robin flying around Rupert's branches now like a crazy bird.

'I thought you had just told me I wouldn't be able to make it in this forest and it didn't sound like you 'trusted me' a few hours ago,' said Rupert smugly.

'You know what I meant, I was just teasing. Of course, I knew you could handle this forest, but I just wasn't sure about the Tree Maaaaa...' Robin stopped talking and pointed at the five tall figures with long spears who had emerged from the darkness.

'Oh, hello Tree Masters, nice to meet you, I have heard so much about you, not necessarily good but the first impressions count and so far so good, you look like a friendly bunch!' Rupert replied with a smile trying to relax the atmosphere but in fact, he felt that he could wet his pants from fear if he had them.

He wasn't sure they enjoyed his sense of humour because they were only standing there, staring at him and Robin with big eyes.

'You have entered the Kingdom of Trepolis, why are you here?' the tallest one asked. He was so tall that a normal human being would fit twice into him.

'We are on our way to find Forest Mother and we just need to pass through your land. I hope it's ok with you? We mean no trouble and we will be out of here as soon as possible if you show us the shortest way?' replied Rupert with confidence trying to hide his shaky from fear branches.

'You have entered it without asking for permission. You are on land which does not belong to you,' the tall man replied.

'Well, to be honest, how should I know this is your land? It's not like you had a border check or something?' replied Rupert.

'There is a sign. Didn't you see it?' the man replied with slight annoyance.

'What sign? You mean this little plaque on the tree?' Rupert pointed at a small sign which said something like shwoapaiekelw in a language that he did not understand.

'How could I have known it's your border when it's written in some gibberish gibber blabla? If you wrote it in English...now that would be a different story.'

'Ok, Mr. Jokey Tree, what exactly do you want here?' the man asked.

'We just need to peacefully walk through your territory so that I can speak to the Forest Mother who put a spell on me and in fact also on the woman I love. Do you know what I mean by... love?'

'I see, well if it's about love, we shall help you. There isn't much in this life that's more important than love. We will escort you to the other side of our land, even though I don't think you should speak to Forest Mother. She isn't very friendly towards visitor oaks. I heard she much prefers handsome pine trees if you know what

I mean but maybe her sentiments have changed,' he replied with a cheeky smile.

'Right, I am not here for anything romantic with her so stop joking. Now, I don't have a lot more time to waste on chit chats.. let's go.'

'Hey, Robin,' whispered Rupert a moment later.

'Yaaaasss,' he replied cheerfully, knowing that now they had nothing to worry about since the Tree Masters had turned out to be very friendly.

'Can you see this lion? Or that bear?' asked Rupert in a low voice.

'What do you mean? What lion? What bear? Stop playing silly games with me, Rupi, it's not the right time to scare me again.'

'Look, these moss and ivy formations, they are shaped like a lion over there and a bear right there, and... I can even see... oh my God, a badger,' Rupert whispered back.

'Oh them, umm, well maybe they got turned into moss and ivy for walking into their land without permission?'

'What? Are you serious?' asked Rupert more and more worried, moving slowly with his roots behind Tree Masters and looking around trying to understand what this was all about.

'I think they are very nice, it's just when they get angry they turn animals into this. Luckily you are a tree and they won't turn you into it, and after all, what could they turn you into if you are already full of moss and ivy most of the time,' replied Robin bursting out laughing.

'Oi, that's not funny, it's a dirty job walking in a blooming forest as a tree you know,' replied Rupert with a louder voice this time, agitated by Robin's remarks.

'I know my friend, I know, don't worry, I think we will be just fine here,' replied Robin he looked around once more, staring at the formations which were still like the stone and a sudden chill went down his spine, 'I just wonder what they did to quacking end up like this...' he added.

They all then disappeared into the depths of the dark forest, hopeful for the bright future ahead.

Chapter 21

FOREST MOTHER

That horrible witch that had turned me into the tree couldn't possibly be more beautiful.

She was gorgeous. Ok, not as gorgeous as Amara, my true love, but she was stunning. When I entered the moss-covered wooden fortress guarded by giant silver wolves with big red shining eyes and paws as big as my biggest roots, I was in awe of the beauty surrounding me. 'If she is a gorgeous woman living in such a beautiful place, why did she play tricks on me and with my life?' I thought. Her long hair was blond and glowed in the candlelight. Her silhouette was of a perfect Goddess. Dressed in a dark green gown with long sleeves and a very revealing deep décolletage and sprinkled with leaves, she stepped down from the top of wide stairs when I had entered the massive hallway with chandeliers made of fireflies, shaped like flower vases. On her right shoulder, a raven was sitting still but staring at me with its black piercing eyes. Its beak was long and crooked, not the kind of bird I would want to make angry or have as my enemy.

'Well, well, well,' she started in a pleasant but a firm voice, 'You have finally found me,' she continued and pierced me right through my thick bark with her glowing big green eyes. I wasn't sure if I found them scary or just attractive.

'Yes, I have finally found you,' I replied with confidence and a sense of achievement of this 'mission impossible' as Robin and others had tried to tell me, 'I found you now and I can see you are not even surprised. You know who I am?' I continued.

'Of course, I know you, my dearest Rupert,' I have watched you since you were a little boy when you visited this forest with your father, the king. I have cared for you and watched over you every time the storm was about to unfold and you were in danger of not making it back to the castle on time. I stopped the lightning from striking you, and wild animals from eating you alive. Of course, you don't remember any of this and probably don't even appreciate it now that you know. I have done more for you than you can imagine,' she replied with a smooth, seductive voice that gave me shivers down my trunk.

'Oh, is that so? If that's the case, how come you turned me with such hatred into this.. this..? I snapped at her, unable to hold my anger and frustration anymore.

'My dearest,' she started replying but I interrupted her, 'Please, stop this unnecessary fake politeness. You obviously hate me, that's why you turned me into this. You must have hated me to do such a cruel thing. So all I am asking you to do now is to just remove this spell and let's finish with this nightmare!' I exclaimed.

'You think I did it because I hate you? Oh well, I have to tell you that you are wrong,' she replied, getting dangerously close to me, touching my bark with her left hand which gave me unexpected shivers, 'my dearest Rupert, I did it because of love,' she continued.

'Love? Don't be ridiculous. What has love got to do with it?' I interrupted but she kept moving closer and closer until she wrapped both of her arms around me and I could feel her heartbeat. I didn't know what was happening to me, it was the most electrifying experience of my life. I couldn't move, I could hardly breathe and my juices were flowing in all my wooden parts as if I was about to explode.

'What are you doing to me?' I mumbled not wanting to be in this situation any longer but she kept squeezing me tighter and tighter, making my thinking foggy and blurred. I was feeling so dizzy that I worried I was about to faint and collapse which would be embarrassing in front of an attractive woman.

'I love you Rupert' she whispered, making me even dizzier with the whole world around me swirling in a huge vortex.

'What did she mean by 'she loved me' like she actually loved me??' I thought.

'I love you and I want to be happy with you for the rest of my life, for hundreds of years and more...I want you. Your love, your heart, and your soul. And I know you want it too. Because you have always wanted to find true love. I knew I was the only one who could give it to you. I just needed you to finally find me. It was the only way. Please forgive me. It was the only way to keep you in this forest and make you come and find me. You wouldn't have done it otherwise. I had to let you know about my existence. I had to do this. But now you know the truth, I know you will forgive me, right Rupert?' she replied again in a silky smooth voice, looking up into my eyes with sparkles in hers and a delicate smile on her juicy red lips.

I couldn't believe what I was hearing and seeing. I couldn't believe that's what it was all about.

'So you did this to me because you..loved me? This horrible act of taking away my human body and existence so I can find you? I wasn't expecting to hear that I must say. That's not what

I wanted to hear and that's not why I am here,' I replied firmly having regained control over my blurred thoughts.

'I understand Rupert, it's a bit of a shock to you but that's the truth. Look at me. I have this kingdom. I rule all kingdoms. I am the Queen of the Forest. The whole of nature belongs to me. I have been only missing one thing all my life. YOU. But now that you have finally made it, I can tell you this; we can be finally happy now. Together forever,' she added loosening up her embrace and stepping away so I could finally breathe freely.

'No!' I replied.

'What do you mean, no?'

'No, I will not stay here with you forever and ever. I don't love you. I only love one woman on Earth.'

'Oh, don't tell me you fell in love with that silly Amara. She is just a distraction, an unnecessary stumbling block and a bait that was eventually going to lead you to me.'

'Oh, no no no, she is the one and only woman I love and want to be with. And I have come here to ask you to take the spell off me and her because we cannot be together for as long as I am a tree and she is a dryad that you turned her into.'

'I never turned her into a dryad you silly, she has always been one. From the moment you turned into the oak. Each oak has its own dryad and unfortunately, that was something I could do nothing about. The only thing I did was to give her a sip of the water from the lake which made her forget who she truly was and made her think she was just a girl living as an orphan in a forest. That's all. But you were never meant to fall in love with her. Because she isn't your true love. I am,' she replied and started moving away from me slowly, step by step backwards without leaving my eyesight.

'My offer for you is simple. You will be back to being your human self if you stay here with me to love me forever. I also promise I shall turn Amara into a human being too so that she can find love with someone else. So, what do you say?'

'I say... thank you very much but I will not accept your offer. I love Amara,' I replied.

She kept smiling and her movements made me feel uncertain of what would happen next. Her silhouette was a perfect shape, her demeanour seemed majestic but tense at the same time. When she finally stopped by the long wooden table dressed in candelabras in the corner of the chamber, she sat on the beautifully carved tall chair. The light from the big fireplace made her skin sparkle. Her neck, her cheeks, her breasts. She then started to slowly unfasten the dress just below the belly button slowly, looking into my eyes relentlessly, making my juices flow even faster into every branch. She then stood up and with her both hands she gently removed the sleeves and both sides of her dress, unveiling her perfect naked body right in front of me. She sat on the chair and crossed her legs on the table, continuing to stare at me.

'This is yours Rupert,' she finally spoke with a delicate smile, 'this can be all yours. If you want it. But you have to say 'yes'. That's all. You just need to say 'yes,' she continued in the most seductive voice I had ever heard.

'I, I...' I muttered wanting to say something but I was unable, looking at the most unexpected vision of my life.

'What's wrong Rupert, don't you want..this? Don't you want all this to be yours?'

'I, I.. no, I don't. . . ' I mumbled.

She reached out for the wooden cup on the table and poured red wine into it from an engraved wooden jar. She put it close to her mouth, continuing to look right into my eyes, took a long sip of wine and then spilled some of it onto her bare, shining from the fire, breasts, making it flow down her belly button and her right thigh, turning herself into the most delicious looking female body ever.

'Whoops, silly me, look I spilled such a good wine. What shall we do about it?' she replied with a bigger smile this time which, however, soon disappeared having heard no response from me.

She lifted herself up, standing tall and dripping with red wine.

'You see Rupert, if you were mine you could help me with this mess I have made. As a man you could. And you still can but only if you stay with me forever.' she said confidently.

I was so overwhelmed by the vision that I didn't just know what to say. I mean, I knew what I wanted to say. I wanted to say that's all for nothing but I knew I had to be gentle. I knew I was put in a situation which may be very difficult to deal with but I had to try. I had to fight for my love, my true love, Amara and it was my one and only chance.

'Umm,I really appreciate what you are saying to me right now my dear Forest Mother,' I started in an official voice, 'but I cannot and I shall not be with you forever because, because I don't love you. I love Amara,' I replied, relieved to be finally able to say how I really felt.

She snapped her fingers and turned around. Her naked back was glowing, making her look like a creature out of this world. Her buttocks were firm and shapely. For a second I thought that if I hadn't loved Amara, she really could be a perfect woman for me. Scary woman. But oh, so perfect. She reached out for the silver knife stuck into the wooden table. Its handle was sparkling because it seemed to have been encrusted with diamonds and rubies, the whole handle. She looked at me and then swiftly cut the back of her palm with it making a wide cut dripping with blood and threw the knife on the floor.

'There, that's what I am ready to do to show you I love you. I would die for you. Would you do the same for me in return?' she asked without leaving my eyesight.

'I, I...' I started to mumble but she turned around again and walked up to what seemed like a pool. She slowly stepped onto it. The candles all around it turned her skin a wonderful shade. She kept walking into it until she was completely submerged.

'Oh no, where is she? Did she drown?' I thought but after a while I saw her emerging back onto the opposite side of it, as if she was reborn.

Her naked wet body was glistening in candlelight even more, making my heart beat faster, even though I didn't want it to. Her long hair was now perfectly merged with her wet back and when she stood on the other side she looked at me with her palms facing up. The huge cut on her hand was gone. But how? How could it just disappear? What kind of water was this? To heal and to turn back time? Was it some kind of magic water? I wanted to ask but I said nothing thinking that maybe it was best not to have further conversations.

'I think it's the water from the lake of life,' whispered Robin into my ear, who had been hidden all this time between my branches, 'I heard that it gives enormous powers to anyone who bathes in it. But they say that if you are a good spirit, it enhances your good powers and if you are an evil spirit it enhances your evil powers.'

'Now that explains why she had so much power over me and Amara,' I whispered back, not wanting to let her know I was talking to a bird in my bush.

Her two servant ravens swiftly brought her a green coat and covered her wet, naked body. She kept moving away from me, stepping back on the wide steps and sat on the throne made of wood which, upon a closer look, seemed to be made of.. oak. Two faces of men were carved on each top and it looked as if two men were stuck in an oak throne. I shivered from the sudden realisation that it may end badly for me now.

'I understand that your decision is final Rupert?' she asked with a serious tone in her voice. She stopped smiling and her face turned pale.

'Umm, yees,' I replied, uncertain whether it was still the right thing to say. After all, rejecting her and asking for mercy at the same time was probably not the best idea.

'In that case, we have nothing else to say to each other. I gave you a chance but you rejected me. I gave you a chance for freedom, to go back to your human self and everlasting love with me. I understand that this will not happen because you don't want it. So I suggest you go now. We are done here,' she replied with a cold and merciless voice.

'What do you mean I can go? Go where?'

'Go back to the forest.'

'You mean as I am now? You won't help me and turn me back into a human again?'

'That's exactly right,' she replied, squeezing both palms into fists as if this decision was not comfortable for her.

'Oh, no,no,no, you can't do that! You don't understand,' I replied frantically.

'I understand perfectly well. I am simply not good enough for you Rupert, am I? You don't want to be with me. In that case, you shall stay as you are forever. Don't worry I won't turn you into my throne. These two really deserved it but I will be merciful to you and let you go. But you shall stay as you are forever. A sad miserable oak, unable to make Amara happy' she said in a heartless voice that almost froze my heart, if I had one.

'Oh, noo, please don't do it,' I begged. You cannot do it. I really love Amara and I want to be with her for as long as I live. Please free us both from the spell.'

'What spell are you talking about Rupert? There is no spell on Amara. She is your dryad. Your tree nymph. It's only natural they are born into every oak in this forest. I have already told you. It was just unfortunate that you fell in love with her. It was never my plan. You were never supposed to fall in love with her!' she now exclaimed in anger and frustration, and stood up.

'So she is really my dryad?' I asked, feeling more and more petrified.

'You fool! Yes, she is your bloody dryad and she shall live for as long as you live, which... I shall do now. Only because I am merciful to you. I like you. I loved you but now I only like you and you are free to live as you wish. But I will not turn you back into a human. It will be your punishment for rejecting me!' she exclaimed and started laughing until hundreds of ravens on the beams of the chamber flew away, swooshing their wings around her and me, turning the whole space into the whirlwind of scary darkness. I felt like fainting and closed my eyes.

I made a wish for this nightmare to be over.

Chapter 22

MOONLIGHT DANCE

The gilded room, or rather a majestic hall of the sandstone castle on a hill, covered in paintings and mirrors reflecting hundreds of candlelight chandeliers shaped like giant crystal crowns, was a perfect spot for an engagement ball of Prince Henri of Fardom and Amara.

They had only met a while ago when Prince Henri was riding through the forest and having noticed Amara he asked her what she was picking and putting into her basket. It was an encounter that turned into a great attraction from his side and he proposed to her on the steps of his castle days later.

She said: 'Yes'.

'Are you happy my dear?' asked Henri leading her into the middle of the room for the first dance, holding her hand in a long, pink silk glove, perfectly matching her pink lace dress which changed into colours of the rainbow with her every move.

'Yes my prince, I am,' she replied, even though her heart was filled with great sadness and pain from losing Rupert. 'This will pass, I am sure I will soon forget about this moody, unreliable, rude man, or a tree rather,' she thought as she was twirling around looking at the joyful faces of the crowd dressed in colourful clothes and feathers in their hair as if they were birds at a forest party, just less classy.

'I care about you so much Amara, you are the most beautiful woman I have ever seen, I love you and I cannot wait to marry you,' said Prince Henri just as they had stopped drinking champagne from crystal glasses with two handles shaped like swans.

For some inexplicable reason, Amara found the swans very comforting. She didn't really know why she couldn't stop staring at them.

'I know, and I cannot wait to marry you and be finally happy,' she replied, smiling shyly and looking into his sparkling eyes even though her heart was screaming from pain.

Henri was a very handsome, well-built young prince with blond hair and blue eyes, a dream man for many noble ladies and princesses. He was charming, dressed impeccably and his manners were perfect. He knew how to dance and how to charm with beautifully sounding words. He was the perfect man. Amara felt that she couldnt have found a better prince in the whole Universe, especially since she wasnt a princess herself.

'I am happy,' she whispered into his ear, trying to convince herself she was doing the right thing but in one of the tall mirrors she saw Rupert peeking through the tall window.

Her heart stopped. She turned around but there was nobody there. 'I think I am going mad,' she thought and continued dancing. When the waltz had stopped, Henri excused her presence and walked up to Lady Sitera who was now blushing from an avalanche of compliments that he was paying to her. Amara walked out to the open terrace through the tall glass and wooden door which were open to the warm and humid night, brightened up only by the bold face of the Moon, only interrupted now and again by small clouds moving quickly in one direction as if they were rushing to a Heavenly Meeting.

She stepped down from the wide stone steps towards the fountain with Greek statues. The music from the hall was gradually fading away and all she could hear were the crickets playing their goodnight sonata and the sound of the water splashing in the gigantic fountain of the powerful Neptune and his entourage.

'Rupert, why did you leave me? Why?' she thought as she sat on the white bench looking as if white lace was embroidered into the brass. She closed her eyes and tears started flowing down her cheeks. 'I am getting married tomorrow to the most handsome prince in all kingdoms and I am feeling… sad. I cannot feel this way. It's not right. I should be joyful and happy,' she thought but when she looked at the castle she could see Henri dancing now with Lady Mildred, laughing and enjoying himself.

'I am so sorry,' she heard a whisper, 'I didn't want to hurt you but you know why I cannot be with you,' the familiar voice continued.

When she turned around she saw Rupert, standing there with his roots out and leaves pointing to the ground as if he had dried out from the amount of time he spent walking and not being rooted to take in the nutrients he needed to survive.

'What, what are you doing here?' she whispered back.

'I have come to say that, umm…' he continued.

'What… what do you want to say? I think you said enough last time you told me to get away from you. You told me you don't love me and I should find another man,' she replied.

'Yes, I mean, no. I mean I can't love you Amara, you know that! I am only a tree. I can't give you what you need. You deserve to be happy with someone like Henri. He seems to be a good man.'

'Yes, maybe he is a good man,' she muttered but with very little conviction, her voice breaking from emotion.

'Maybe? Do you have any doubts about it?' asked Rupert in a low voice.

'No, of course not, I am sure that he is and that he will be a good husband. He will look after me and Runo. And I am sure that when we get married he will spend more time with me than with other ladies. He is just enjoying his last night before getting married tomorrow and dances with everyone,' she mumbled.

'Umm, are you sure he is going to be different after the wedding? I heard that men don't change but that's just me, don't listen to me. I am just a tree. What do I know?'

'Well, men do change and they have to change when they get married. It's a new situation for them and they need to adjust. I will make him so happy he won't even look at other ladies! But you are right, maybe I am fooling myself. Maybe I shouldn't expect him to change, maybe this is all a big fat lie and I shouldn't marry him,' Amara replied.

'Oh, don't say that, I want you to be happy, I am sure he will give you the happiness you deserve, what life would you have with me?'

'Well, we could live happily ever after in the forest but you don't want that. You are pushing me into the arms of another man.'

'Yes exactly, a man who isn't a tree and who can give you a marriage and family that you deserve,' said Rupert and started to move away, one root at a time. 'But there is something I need you to know,' he whispered,' I love you. I always will. I just want you to know that.'

'Really? You love me? How can you say you love me? You don't want me, you tell me to be with another man and now I don't believe a word you say now. When you truly love someone, you don't push them away and tell them to find happiness with someone else,' replied Amara with tearful eyes shining bright in the reflecting moonlight.

'No matter what I say, my love for you always has been, always is, and always will be. The clouds in the sky will move in all directions possible, the wind will bend and twist my branches, toss and remove all my leaves in the autumn, the cold snowflakes will cover my whole being, the night will constantly change into days but my love for you will remain unshaken. I will always be here for you, no matter where you go, no matter if you leave to follow your path, no matter if you come to me tomorrow or in one thousand years. My love for you will always BE in me and it will last for an eternity. For as long as I live as an oak, that's how long I will love you. I know it because I feel it with every molecule of my body and I have never been more certain of anything in my entire life. No human being will change it, no vicious animal will bite and prevent me, no storm will tear me apart and no lightning strike can make me stop. I will stop when my heart stops beating in this tree and...'

'And..?' she whispered.

'And it will last forever and ever until the beginning and the end of the Universe when we will finally meet, until you finally understand that we are destined to be together and find each other as twin flames, once split from one soul into two and now searching for each other. We are meant to be together once we have learnt all we need to learn to grow separately as souls and then unite again in eternal love, bigger than you can imagine, stronger than any forces of nature. We will be together, it's only up to you to realise it and decide when. I already know that. But until you are ready to love me as much as I love you, I will wait. By our river bench and I will not move. I will be here for you. For as long as I breathe, for as long as I live. Forever and always. Because to me no flower can compare to your beauty, no star in the sky can compare to the beauty of your soul,' said Rupert.

'Is love when you say you leave the one you love for their own good or is love when you stay regardless of circumstances? Maybe when you make a decision to love then there is no compromise and no way back. No way to retreat and take everything back, to leave as if nothing had happened? Maybe when you love you love forever and everything else is just one big lie? After all, love is the feeling of joy, compassion and happiness shown to your beloved and not the lack of it. How can the lack of love mean love? I just don't understand it,' said Amara after listening to Rupert's confession and sat down on the rock, feeling her knees getting shaky.

She needed a moment or two to think about what he had just said. She believed him and she could feel his love and compassion, so why was she so resistant to saying to him that she loved him too. With all her heart and soul, did she really want to marry Prince Henri? And live Happily Ever After in his castle? Was that what she wanted? Her thoughts were running around like lost hares in the forest. She stood up and took a deep breath.

'Rupert, I...' she whispered but stopped when Rupert took her hand gently in his branch and said; 'Would you honour me with the last dance together?' and put his other branch on her back.

They then gently swayed to the sound of Waltz coming through the open windows of the castle in the distance, looking at each other's eyes, and in that moment, Amara felt as if she was truly dancing with Prince Rupert, the charming, gentleman that he was, despite his current appearance. It wasn't easy for Rupert to move to the rhythm because his roots were constantly in the way and he wanted to make sure he didn't step on Amara's silver slippers. At that moment they both forgot about the whole world. Amara became tearful and when she looked at the Moon that had just peeked from under a big white cloud she shed a tear. 'Don't cry my lady, everything will be as it should be, you will find your love and happiness, just not with me, trust me, you will.'

'What if I don't? I don't want to lose you. You are my best friend, you are my peace, you are the one I can always go to and just be myself, here in this forest. What if my perfect marriage isn't going to be like this? I am fearful Rupert. I am torn and as much as I want to listen to you and settle down with Henri I am not sure he will give me what you can give me.'

'I am just an ugly oak and how could anyone love me? For who I am? I am just a bloody tree. But if you do have any feelings for me, then please do tell me, and even if you don't, I will still love you, because you are LOVE, you are every blade of grass covered in the morning dew, you are every hilltop lit up in the sunrise, you are part of this Universe and you are part of me. It does not matter if you don't love who I have become for I have become who I have deserved to become. All that matters is that you know! That I love YOU and who you are. With all your imperfections which only make you perfect. You are the most beautiful and caring woman I have ever met. For me, you are the image of perfection. For me, you are LOVE, and even if you get angry even if you shout at me, even if you slap my branches in frustration, you are the woman I want to love for the rest of my days. I want to love you for a thousand years and more. My love for you is as strong as when the Moon kisses the Sun for good morning and goodnight every time they touch passing by and become one for one split second but my love is like this all the time. I never believed in fate before but now I know it was fate that had brought us together. You are my fate, you are my Sun and my Moon and I want to love you for eternity and make you happy but I cannot because...' Rupert stopped his confession thinking that he had heard someone coming but looked around and having seen nobody he continued, 'Apart from unconditional love I cannot give you anything else. I am sorry I have come to confuse you even more. I am sorry I rejected you out of fear. I am sorry I have come here at all, I shouldn't have,' replied Rupert and released both of her arms. 'Please, take my acorn as a sign of my love for you and my everlasting devotion to you. Always keep it near you and when you feel you need me, when you are in danger, squeeze it tight in your hand and think of me. I will immediately know you need me. I will come and find you. It will be our connection forever and ever. I will always be here for you. We are connected through this acorn now,' he added, placing it in the palm of her hand.

Amara heard clear footsteps of someone approaching from the castle and turned around.

'My dearest Amara, I have been looking for you everywhere! Darling, who are you talking to?' she heard the familiar voice of Henri.

'Nobody my dear, I was just talking to a tree...' she replied but stopped finishing the sentence while looking at Rupert's eyes. 'I was just thinking out loud, repeating the vows for our wedding,' she continued.

'What? Talking to a tree? Oh my dear, why would you talk to a tree? They don't understand you and they are big, clumsy, and ugly stupid creatures, like this one here, look,' he replied pointing at Rupert and leaning against him in a stretch.

'They do understand us, they understand me,' Amara objected, 'trees have feelings just like you and me. They are wise because they are connected with the whole Universe and their energy is very calming and healing. They can even love,' she added smiling at Rupert's surprised face.

'Oh dear, you drank too much champagne. I'm afraid to tell you that they are just bloody trees, ugly, especially this one, I don't really remember it being here, ummm, I need to speak to my gardener in the morning and tell him to cut it and use it as logs for the castle fireplaces. Anyway, enough of talking about stupid trees,' he replied in an arrogant voice.

'Why? I love them, they have saved my life many times in the forest, I could climb on top of them when I was in danger from wild wolves and they gave me shelter and comfort when I needed it. I never felt alone when I was with them, not like with humans, you never know if they are honest and trustworthy, they pretend to be your friend but when you turn around they stab you in the back, telling stories which are untrue and hateful. That's what I heard from the hares and squirrels anyway. I loved growing up among the trees. They were my friends. I think if you spend more time in the forest, you will love them as much as I do.'

'I don't think so darling, I am planning to build two more hunting lodges in the forest and I have already ordered the cutting down of some of the oldest, crooked and miserable-looking trees. I need space for the huge buildings and they will be then used to make furniture, to cover the walls and be used in the fireplaces. You will love them, trust me, they will be perfect getaway houses for us. We can then go fox and hare hunting. I will get you the most flattering leather hunting outfit to wear. There are so many things I want to do with you. I can't wait to marry you tomorrow,' he replied and grabbed Amara by the waist, pulled her towards him, and placed a forceful kiss on her lips which she didn't find appealing at all.

Rupert's heart sank watching this but he knew he couldn't move. He watched the love of his life being kissed by another man and he knew there was nothing more for him to live for. He knew he was going to die as a sad, lonely tree with nobody to ever love him, he knew that because Forest Mother told him so, he knew she would never take the spell back. He knew his life as a human was over because if he turned into a human, Amara would die. He could never give her what she needed. He knew he could never kiss Amara passionately in the moonlight again just like he did on the boat on the lake in the magical part of the forest which she didn't even remember. He knew it was going to be torture for him for as long as he lived, which could easily be a few thousand years.

He also hoped that Amara could never find out about it and the sacrifice he had made for her.

She wouldn't have let him make that sacrifice.

For him, it was the choice of love.

Love for her.

Chapter 23

ACORN

When the party was over, Amara went to her top floor bedroom in the right-wing of the castle which was now filled with warm candlelight.

A fresh breeze gently swayed the blue silk curtains letting in the fresh forest air filled with the scent of her beloved oakmoss, reminding her of Rupert. He always smelled of it because it grew on him. He was always annoyed about fungi being stuck on his parts but she found it adorable. She lay down on the cotton bedsheets but she couldn't fall asleep, feeling hot and worrying about the wedding ceremony the next day, unable to stop thinking about Rupert, their last dance, and his words for her. 'If he truly loves me then why doesn't he want to be with me? It just doesn't make sense,' she kept asking herself in her head over and over again, unable to fall asleep.

She then heard dogs barking in the distance so she stepped onto the small terrace and looked at the gardens and the forest behind them which was shimmering in bright moonlight. She enjoyed the feeling of the cooling night breeze wrapping her naked body underneath the long white silk gown and she was dreaming of a miracle to happen. A miracle to magically turn Rupert back into a prince so that he could come and get her on his dark horse, kidnap her into the sunset, ride fast without stopping and without caring what the world might think of them.

When she noticed tiny lights flickering behind the trees, she decided to go towards them. Curious, she was running fast down the stone spiral staircase, hardly visible at dimmed candlelight. When she approached the lights behind tall trees she froze and her heart sank. Hundreds of deer with huge antlers were being forced into wooden wagons by the guards holding fire lanterns. The deer did it without any objection, one after another as if hypnotised. Henri was sitting on a horse, watching and supervising the whole process.

'Off with them, next!' he commanded, 'I want them all. I want their antlers and their skins ready for tomorrow morning. Bring them back to me,' he shouted in a cruel voice that she had never heard before.

Amara stood there unable to move, trying to understand what was truly happening until she had finally realised that the man she was about to marry tomorrow was killing the deer of the forest for their skin and antlers. When Henri looked in her direction, she knew he noticed her and that it was the end of her. She knew she was witnessing the biggest monster this forest had seen and she was in huge danger. She turned around and ran, losing her silver slippers along the way. She started running on cold humid grass back to the castle, hurting her bare feet. She knew she had to run away from him. She knew she had to save herself and the deer. Breathless, after climbing up what had seemed like a thousand steps up the spiral staircase, she locked her chamber and quickly put on her old dress with the leather corset that she used to wear in the forest. She heard Henri following her all this time and now he was banging loudly on her door, making it shake from the sheer force of his fists.

'How could you do this? Why are you doing this?' she exclaimed through the door.

'Darling, it's not what you think it is. It is only a relocation project. We have too many deer in the forest. They will be moved to other kingdoms, that's all.'

'You are lying! You are a cruel man! I heard you saying you want their antlers and skin in the morning!'

'No darling, it's not true, you misheard. Please open the door so we can talk.'

Amara opened the door not because she wanted to see Henri but because she wanted to hear from his own lips what this was all about before she would make a final decision.

'You are killing those deer. Why? I ask you, why?'

'Ok, ok, calm down, I am not killing them.'

'Yes you are, I heard you giving orders. I am not stupid. I should have known better. I should have known you are not a good man after all, how could I have been so stupid!' she continued believing her own eyes and ears more than Henri's words, 'I will not marry you tomorrow. Can you hear me? I will not. I prefer to be alone forever than with a cruel man like you, killing the most precious animals of this forest. I hate you, I hate you!' she exclaimed with tearful eyes. Her cheeks were red from running and extreme anger.

'Ok, well that didn't go down well. I'd never thought you would be such a drama queen just because of some stupid deer or two. Ok then, yes, you are right. I do kill them. Because I need to make money to keep this luxurious castle and provide all the jewels to you, now that I am marrying you. Where do you think all this wealth comes from? I either kill people to steal their possessions or I kill stupid deer to sell to people who pay a lot of money for their skin and antlers. It's not an easy choice to make. But you have helped me with the latter. The deer come to me from the whole kingdom because they trust you and your love for them. You are so sweet and naive but they love you. I only needed you for that. To attract them to me, walking perfectly right into the trap. That's the truth. Happy now?' he replied with a vicious and angry look.

'Yes, I am happy to know the truth about who you are,' she replied and pushed Henri out of the doorway and closed it with the key.

She then quickly grabbed the only precious thing she could think of taking and put it in her pocket. She ran into the balcony and started sliding down the vines helping her along the way to free herself from the prison she had put herself in.

She rushed into the depths of the forest and squeezed one thing that was the most important of all the treasures of that castle.

The acorn.

She looked into the sky which, in spite of the deep night, was illuminated by half a moon and white clouds reflecting its light.

'Rupert, I need you. Please come to me. Where are you? I need your help,' she whispered, staring at the sky which seemed so vast and powerful with clouds gliding gently in the moonlight as if arranging into a pattern. She blinked her eyes because she couldn't believe what she was seeing. There was hardly any breeze on her skin that she could feel and the clouds were moving. She opened her eyes again and she saw Rupert's face made up of clouds, looking at her in the most loving, caring way she could imagine. It was him. She knew he could hear her cry for help. She knew it and there couldn't be a clearer sign. She then heard a whisper from his lips; 'I will come and get you. I will come and find you. I love you.'

Tears started flowing down her cheeks because it was the most magical way of hearing she was truly loved and it was all true. It melted her heart from joy but at the same time the pain of being so far away from him, worrying how he would find her in the middle of the dark forest. 'I...I...' she started whispering back but she heard loud barking and howling getting closer. She looked around and she could see flickering lights of the fire lanterns of the guards with their wild beasts, which had red flashing eyes, moving towards her with big thumps that made the ground under her feet shake. She looked up into the sky but Rupert's face was gone. Running into the darkness of the forest along the river bank with all her strength and power, she kept squeezing the acorn in her right palm, feeling as if it had become part of her. She was scared. She was petrified. She didn't know if Rupert would make it on time to come and rescue her. The howling of the wild wolf beasts was now right behind her. The guards were shouting louder and louder; 'Get her! I can see her! She is right there!' Amara turned around for the last time to look at their vicious faces, illuminated by the fire lanterns of the evil men on horses. She then felt the sharp paws of a wild beast on her back, sliding down her dress, ripping it in half. She then lost her balance, tripping over a root, and fell with full force onto the ground. Another beast grabbed her arm. All she could feel was a sharp pain in her left shoulder and she knew she was about to die now, ripped into pieces. She squeezed the acorn even more.

'Leave her!' a familiar voice of the man she hated so much now could be heard among the loud puffing and growling.

She felt her hair being pulled to the back and the man she despised so much looked into her face, illuminating it with the fire lantern.

'And where do you think you are going?' he said in a nasty voice which gave her shivers, 'I never said you are allowed to go anywhere. We are getting married tomorrow. Remember?' he continued breathlessly from the chase and with the confidence of a madman.

'I am not going back with you. I despise you!' she exclaimed and spat into his face but she regretted that a second later because of the massive pain of being lifted up from the ground by her hair.

'Leave me alone! I will not marry you! I hate you for what you have done. You kill innocent deer. You shall pay for that! And I will not help you with your plan. I will not, can you hear me!?' she exclaimed with the confidence of a woman who had nothing more to lose other than her life.

'My dear Amara, how naive are you. You think you can just run away from me and all will be fine. Back to where? Living in a shed in a forest? I helped you get out of it. You had nothing and I still wanted to marry you, remember? But you don't appreciate it now? Well, that's not very nice, is it? You ungrateful...' he replied with nastiness in his voice, staring at her with his mad eyes adding, 'Ropes!'

One of his men gave him the ropes and Henri twisted her arms and tied her wrists in front of her as if she was his slave now, despite her attempts to fight him. He did it with such strength that she found it hard to hold her pain inside but she didn't scream. She was too proud of that. Having been pushed towards the horse,

Henri mounted her on his black stallion and sat right behind her. Escorted by the guards, they all galloped back to the castle. Amara was grateful for the cold night breeze on her face, neck, and shoulders cooling her body, making it almost numb because she didn't want to feel trapped with the man she would prefer to see dead rather than sitting behind her.

Chapter 24

BUTTERFLY

Having reached the courtyard, Henri dismounted Amara from his horse and pulled her by the rope tied around her wrists towards the cathedral.

She followed him like an animal that was about to be slaughtered, unable to escape its captivity. Having entered the cathedral up the stone steps, Amara felt the softness of the red thick carpet under her bruised and cut from running away feet. The carpet was spread right up to the altar. The air inside was thick and humid, filled with the scent of magnolia and jasmine flowers wrapped all around the tall stone columns and attached to every wooden bench along the long aisle. The candles that were still lit gave a warm feeling to her cold body, almost frozen from the chase and the cold night. For a moment she felt dizzy but she knew she had to stay conscious and strong.

'I have just realised that we haven't practised our vows for tomorrow,' said Henri walking in front of her and pulling the rope mercilessly.

Amara was getting more and more dreamy. She felt as if she was about to faint from the surreal vision of the most beautifully dressed church for her wedding day but with a monster in front of her. The organist seeing Prince Henri and Amara walking down the aisle, surprised by the unexpected scenario and thinking it was a rehearsal before the wedding, quickly started playing the organs in the most dramatic way, forgetting about the wedding tune he was supposed to play the next day. Amara's body shivered to the vibrations of the organs, stumbling and swaying on the red carpet, pulled by Henri. She looked up at the organist. He stopped playing. A deafening silence fell upon them and Henri shouted in a cold voice: 'Leave!' The organist quickly ran down the spiral stone steps and out of the church.

'Right, I guess this is your chance to show me how much you love me,' he said, facing her by the altar but Amara looked at his cruel and hateful eyes, unable to speak.

Henri forced her to repeat the wedding vows and when it came to her saying his name she said; 'And I shall love you, Rupert, for as long as I live,' to which Henri slapped her face making her fall onto the ground.

'Rupert? Who the hell is Rupert? Have you lost your mind, woman? My name is Prince Henri, remember?' he exclaimed when she was looking at him with her nose bleeding. His eyes could kill. 'Stand up! I don't have time for this. I hope you say my name right tomorrow!' he added, pulling her by the rope behind him and walking out of the church into the chilly darkness of the night. He then pushed her without saying a word towards the small door on the left of the High Tower. 'Torch!' he exclaimed angrily to his men standing nearby.

He then pushed Amara through the small dark door but because she seemed very resistant to enter, he went in first and pulled her like a slave by the ropes behind him, illuminating the dark stone steps of the narrow staircase leading downstairs. Amara was getting more and more petrified. She knew her end was coming and that she would never see daylight once this journey to hell finished. But there was no way out now. Rupert didn't rescue her. He didn't help her as he had promised. She knew he had abandoned her and she was all by herself now. When the steps had finished, Henri pushed her into the first open cell. The air there was heavy. She could hardly breathe from fear, running away and the worry of being close to death.

'Come on, get in Amara! It's your new home,' said Henri, trying to push her into the darkness of the scary cell even more.

She fell to the ground and hit her head on the stone floor covered with sharp wheat. She then heard Henri disappearing and leaving her in complete darkness. It gave her a moment to close her eyes and dream of being close to Rupert, safe and happy. Not long later, she heard heavy footsteps again. When she looked up, she saw him putting the torch into the metal holder on the wall. Deafening silence surrounded her body and soul in the darkest time of her life. She sat up and looked around. There was a narrow bed on the side of the cell covered in an old blanket and a small wooden table was right under the tiny crescent-shaped window. Henri stood in front of her. His long black boots were dirty from the muddy chase. She looked up at him. He stared at her from up there with merciless eyes and a sick satisfaction of capturing her.

'Look what I brought you, your favourite goulash. I thought you must be starving from all the excitement of this night,' he said and placed a silver plate on the ground in front of her.

Amara was indeed starving and she knew she needed to stay strong. For herself and for Rupert. She slowly started eating it with a silver spoon. It was a meal she had always liked. It was not easy for her to eat it because of the rope around her wrists.

'Good girl. You like it?' asked Henri standing above her and staring at her as if she was the hungry dog of a master.

Amara didn't reply. She wanted to eat as much as possible to gather strength, not trusting him and doubting his kindness would last very long.

'Have you ever wondered what your favourite dish is made of?' he asked.

'You told me it's from dried wild mushrooms,' she replied quickly in between the desperate act of putting chunks of food filling her mouth.

'Well, I told you that story but it's not actually mushrooms,' he replied and Amara looked at his big eyes of a wild beast piercing her from above, feeling uneasy about the answer he had given her, 'It's actually from your deer friends,' he added and burst out laughing loudly, making Amara spit out any remaining food in her mouth.

'How could you!?' she exclaimed angrily.

'How could I? Well, you had to eat something and this is something we definitely have a lot of. What's the problem? You suddenly don't like your friends?' he asked.

Amara looked down at the plate which was almost empty now, feeling tears swelling up in her eyes at the realisation she had just eaten one of her most beloved creatures of the forest.

'Come!' he said with a smirk, reaching out for her hand but she didn't know why he had said it since her hands were still tied by the rope. 'Ooops sorry, I forgot you are such a naughty girl that you need to be tied up. At least for now,' he added with a ferocious laugh.

He then grabbed her by the waist and pulled her up. They were now standing so close to each other that she could feel his bad breath on her lips. She was close to fainting but she knew she had to be strong.

'Please, forgive my manners. It seems that it wasn't supposed to be like this after all. Now whose fault is that?'- he asked. 'You were supposed to sleep tight tonight, like a little mouse under your duvet, and wake up tomorrow morning ready to walk down the aisle with me. But what did you prefer? Sneaking around the dark forest and seeing things you were not supposed to see. You can only blame yourself, my sweet Amara,' he added, pulling her towards him by her waist, breathing heavily at her cheek, holding it with his hand so tight that she could not turn her head away. 'You will walk that aisle tomorrow anyway, do you understand me? You will marry me tomorrow and you shall stay here for as long as it's needed after the wedding so that you forget about running away. Do you hear me?' he shouted right into her ear until shivers went down her spine, 'Do you understand me, I ask?'

'I will not marry you tomorrow or ever. I will never be with you and I will never love you. You are the cruellest and most evil man I have ever met and my heart and soul will always belong to my one and only true love - Prince Rupert of Deer Wonderland Kingdom. I don't care about you and I never will. I will...' she replied but Henri grabbed her lips and squeezed them so tight that it hurt.

'I don't need you to love me or care for me. All I need you for is getting lots of deer coming to me. That's your only job. But what I care about is that you are loyal to me and stop fantasising about some prince that disappeared a long time ago and is probably dead by now, eaten by the wolves,' he replied, 'I don't expect love from you. I expect obedience.'

'Yes, just like from your beastly wolves! She replied with fury in her voice, 'I will always hate you! I will...' she continued until Henri forced his lips upon hers and kissed her. Unable to free herself from the trap, she bit him in the lower lip.

'You bitch!' he shouted angrily and slapped her in the face making her nose bleed even more, 'You shall pay for that!' he screamed and pushed her onto the wooden table lifting her dress up one layer after another. Amara knew that her end was coming one way or another, unable to fight with her hands tied up, she didn't even scream for help. She knew there was nothing or nobody who could help her now.

'Is that what you are dreaming about with your Rupert, that he can do this to you?' he whispered into her ear whilst running his rough big fingers up the back of her thigh, 'Is that what you want?' he continued moving his fingers between her legs, 'I could have you now you know but why should I? You will be mine tomorrow. I don't like spoiling surprises. I shall visit you in this dungeon after the wedding and I will do anything I want to do with you. Do you understand?' he continued breathing in her jasmine skin scent deeply and then exhaling with mad passion into her right ear. 'And I do hope you are a virgin. Are you?' he asked when Amara was gazing with her tearful eyes at the Moon shining brightly through the small window with bars in it, suddenly remembering the passionate night with Rupert on the boat of the magical forest and replied smiling, 'You wish.'

Hearing that, Henri pushed her with full force from the table onto the ground. She fell with a big thump onto the cold stone wall and hit her head again making it bleed.

'What does that mean? Has Prince Rupert had you? How? He is dead! Impossible!' he shouted walking around her body.

'He isn't dead. We spent the most magical night under the stars in the middle of the lake on a boat. I am already his. I have always been only his and I will always be only his. There is nothing you can do to change it. We are One. We have become One. And he will come and rescue me. He promised me that! And he will never leave me alone with you again!' said Amara, standing up slowly and looking into Henri's eyes with such powerful confidence that he made a step back.

'We shall see about that!' he exclaimed and hit her in her face with such strength that she fell onto the floor once more, losing consciousness.

When she opened her eyes she thought she had died. The darkness was all around her but when she looked up she saw the moonlight peeking through the window. She sat on the floor and started weeping.

'Where are you, Rupert? Why have you abandoned me? You promised me you would always look after me. But you lied. I am all alone now and I shall die alone now. Why did you not rescue me? Why did you lie that you loved me? Why?' she whispered through tears and closed her eyes, swollen from crying and beating eyelids.

When she opened her eyes again she thought she was dreaming. A blue bundle of pulsating light flew into the cell and at first, she couldn't make out what it was. She wiped her tears and the tiny ball of blue light got closer. She reached out her tied-up palms and opened them. The blue light was a butterfly. Its wings were pulsating with the light of changing intensity. She was so happy to see it that her face lit up.

'Do not fret Amara. Rupert loves you. You know that deep in your heart. Don't let your fears put any doubts into it. Do not doubt his love and remember: 'Where there is love there is hope,' said the butterfly in the most heavenly sounding voice and flew away leaving Amara.

Her memories of being with Rupert sneaked out of her eyes and rolled down her cheeks. She was now filled with hope.

Chapter 25

BURNING FOR YOU

When Rupert felt the cry for Amara's help when she was squeezing his acorn, he knew she was in huge danger and that he had to rescue her.

'Come, Robin, we need to find Amara!' he exclaimed to him, sleeping on his branch.

'Oh, what now?' replied Robin in a sleepy voice because he hadn't been home for the last three nights after his wife stood at the door with a frying pan, ready to restructure his wings into angel wings for not letting her know where he was for days.

'Amara, she squeezed my nut. Really hard. It's a sign. She needs my help,' said Rupert, taking his roots slowly out of the ground and getting ready for the journey.

'What the quack? So a woman squeezes your nut and you have to go to her? Aww ok, I get it. No need to tell me more,' he replied winking.

'Robin the Wood! Stop joking or I will tell the pigeons to poo on your house roof.'

'Quack, no, please just not the pigeons, I beg you, that stuff is toxic, I won't be able to remove it for months. So, how can I help you my friend?' he asked with a crescent smile.

'Well, we need to find a way to get to Amara quickly. But how?' asked Rupert and as soon as he did they saw a wagon with two horses moving at a distance.

'Leave it to me,' said Robin, 'They don't call me quacking Robin the Wood for nothing!' he added, 'I command you to abandon this wagon right now!' he announced in a serious voice while landing at the back of the horse, right in front of the old man whose face was stunned from hearing a bird talking to him.

'Whoaaaa!' The old man exclaimed stopping the horses, 'What are you saying to me again?' he mumbled.

'I said, abandon this carriage because we need it for a very important mission. Which in my opinion is mission impossible but hey, things we do for friends, right? So yes, leave now or you will quacking regret it,' continued Robin with a confident voice.

'What do you mean by WE?' the old man asked, even more, stunned while turning his head around as if trying to see other birds.

'WE, meaning Robin the Wood and Me, Prince Rupert of Deer Wonderland Kingdom,' said Rupert in low voice walking up to him, and as soon as he had emerged from the darkness, the old man looked as if he had got a heart attack and slid down the carriage, running into the ferns quicker than the wind that passed through his pants.

'There you have it, I quacking sorted it for you,' said Robin with a cheeky smile.

'Oh you,' giggled Rupert, 'anyway, let's go, there is no time to waste. Let's find Amara!' he added and jumped on the wagon shouting yeeeehaaaa to the horses who were so stunned by the talking and walking tree that they started to gallop like crazy as if trying to get away from him.

'Oh yess baby, that's what I call a ride!' exclaimed Rupert laughing and gazing at Robin flying right next to him, feeling the wind in his leaves and knowing that nothing would stop him now.

'I quacking love it!' said Robin.

When Rupert finally saw the castle at a distance he knew that Amara was in huge danger. He could see smoke and fire overtaking its walls and windows right from the very bottom to the very top.

'Oh no, Robin! The castle is on fire! We need to rescue Amara but where is she? Help me???!!' he exclaimed in despair and Robin, seeing the seriousness of the situation, didn't wait much longer before he flew towards the castle to search for Rupert's beloved woman.

'Here, here!' he shouted as soon as he had approached the burning walls. 'She is in here! She is in that cell!' Robin screamed pointing at the small cell window where all that Rupert could see was the shadow of the woman he loved so much.

'My love, I am here, I shall help you now!' Rupert exclaimed, reaching out for the bars with his branches and pulling them apart with all his power. 'Please, move away Amara, let me do this!' he said knowing that fire could be reaching her, 'Don't worry my love!' I am here!' he repeated and seeing her teary eyes sparkling from the flames all around her gave him strength out of this world. He knew he had to rescue her or he would die from despair himself.

Amara didn't even utter a word and did exactly what Rupert had told her. She moved away from the small cell window. Rupert grabbed the bars and started pulling them apart. His branches caught fire immediately and he could feel an immense pain but he knew he couldn't let go. The pain was becoming unbearable but he did not care about it. Finally, after what had seemed like an eternity, he gathered all his strength and ripped the window apart, together with the walls which crumbled into rubble in front of his eyes releasing even more fire that caught onto him.

'Amara! Amara!' Rupert screamed in pain which was both physical and emotional, 'Amara!' he repeated and saw her silhouette emerging from the smoke and fire and then falling on the ground right in front of him.

'My love, are you ok?' he exclaimed but seeing her face in glowing light lifting herself up slowly from the ground, he sighed from relief.

'I am ok Rupert,' she mumbled, 'But you, but you are on.. fire!' she exclaimed in horror seeing his branches burning.

'Don't worry about me!' said Rupert, 'Go, run to the badgers! Run as fast as you can! I want you to be safe,' he added, seeing Henri's guards getting closer, 'Run, please my love, you will be ok, trust me, I will take care of them!' he replied with love in his eyes.

'I don't want to leave you, please don't let me leave you again!' begged Amara.

'I am not telling you to leave me but to be safe. I shall find you. Trust me,' he said, feeling more and more pain from the burning branches.

'Ok, I will,' she replied and started running as fast as she could into the darkness of the forest.

'Well, well, well, who has honoured us with his visit?' Rupert heard Henri's voice and without even looking at the monster responsible for all this he made a huge swing with his burning branch hoping to hit him but he just missed and a knight on his right cut his burning branch off with one big blow of a sword. Rupert felt a sharp pain but didn't make a sound.

'It's all over Henri, you will not hurt Amara any longer. I thought you were a good man. I thought you could make her happy. I was wrong. You will now pay for your cruelty.'

'Haha, you think you will make me pay? How? I can see that you are not dead but you are an old ugly oak. And you are on fire have you noticed? And being a tree I have bad news for you. It's not looking good,' replied Henri in a nasty voice chuckling at his own cruel sense of humour.

'I don't care. Amara is safe and away from you. That's all that matters!'

'Seize him!' Henri exclaimed angrily and his men started throwing ropes at him. 'You are alone Rupert. Look at my knights. You think you can defeat my army?' he added with a vicious laugh.

At that moment, a tree right behind Rupert came closer to him and stood right next to him. Then another huge oak, almost as big as Rupert stood right next to him on the left. Then a sequoia, huge as a tower of the castle stood right behind. Rupert turned around and saw all the trees uprooting and moving closer to him, emerging from the darkness into the light of the castle on fire.

'Rupert is one of us and if you want to fight him, you will have to fight all of us!' they all exclaimed in a low but strong voice simultaneously.

Henri's face went pale. He hadn't expected to face an army of trees helping Rupert. He hadn't been prepared for this.

'Get them!' he exclaimed from both fear and anger to his men dressed in armour who had gathered behind him.

The battle of the knights and trees had begun. The trees were tall, strong, and unpredictable but they didn't have swords. They could hit a knight dressed in heavy armour with such strength though that he flew high up in the air and fell with a massive thump onto the ground. Dead. But the knights were cutting the trees' branches with huge blows of their swords as if removing their limbs and leaving them more vulnerable to ropes to hold them down and cut them into pieces. The noise of the battle was so loud that the neighbouring villagers woke up and looked through the windows of their huts, not believing their eyes. They were witnessing a fierce battle of the knights and trees that this land had never seen before.

Rupert was fighting bravely with everyone else, using his burning branches to his advantage and knowing that he didn't have much time to win. He knew his life was about to end soon if it was to continue like this but he also knew he had to kill Henri who now got scared and jumped on his horse, trying to run away. Rupert saw him after he had hit another knight into the darkness with full force and he knew he had to kill the man who was a deadly danger to his love.. to is Amara. He approached Henri and screamed; 'Where do you think you are going?' But before Henri had a chance to reply he hit him with full force, making him fall off the horse with a loud thump into the mud. Henri reached out for the sword and started fighting Rupert, cutting his branches with every blow Rupert made, leaving him with almost nothing to fight with.

'I am not going anywhere you cripple! Look at you! You are all bare. You have burnt and lost your branches. You can do nothing to me anymore!'

'Yes, I caaa...' Rupert tried to reply but before he was able to finish the word, he felt ropes all around him, stopping him from moving and the more he tried to move, the more he was losing his balance.

He then fell with a big thump onto the ground knowing that his end was close now. 'It's over for me. It really is' he thought but just as he did he heard loud thunder and when he opened his eyes, the most powerful light hit him with such strength that he thought he had died and gone into Heaven. But to his surprise, he felt the most unearthly strength and he lifted himself up again. The thought of leaving Amara in the hands of this dangerous man would not let him rest in peace and the Universe was helping him. He knew he had to live, he knew he had to survive. For her. Because he loved her.

'You will never defeat me!' exclaimed Rupert with fierce eyes staring at Henri who stood there and couldn't believe what he was seeing, amazed by the strength of Rupert's will to live and the lightning that had struck him, giving him that power.

Rupert then turned his back on Henri to see if the battle was almost over and in that very moment a net of strong ropes fell upon him once more, making it impossible for him to move.

He knew it was the end of him.

He knew it was the end for both of him and Amara.

He knew he had lost.

Chapter 26

EAGLE WINGS

Amara was running with all her strength through the petrifying darkness of the forest towards the wooden bench by the river that Rupert had made for her by cutting through a log, and which was close to the badgers.

The thickness of the vicious ferns catching her bare feet and sticks hurting them with every step only made her more determined to make it to the safe place. She knew Rupert would be fine and he would come and get her just as he had promised. Once she got to the river she saw the bench and the Moon was showing her the way. She recognised the lights in the little windows of their little hut covered in moss and knocked on the door.

'Rupert, it's Rupert, he rescued me from the castle and stayed there. He told me to come here to wait for him,' she hardly mumbled, breathless from running so fast.

'Oh poor child, take a seat and rest, tell me all about it,' said Emily with a loving voice and seated Amara on the rock by the river. Amara told her what had happened.

'Oh no, that's awful, so did Rupert say he would come and get you? Are you sure he is fine?' asked Emily, visibly worried.

'Yes that's what he said,' repeated Amara but with a voice that was now lacking confidence.

She then stood up and walked along the river looking at the water surface glistening in the moonlight. She stepped onto the little wooden bridge and stared at the reflection of the Moon in the ripples which seemed to be now moving faster and faster until Rupert's face appeared in them. She knew it was a sign. She knew she had to do something. She couldn't just sit there and do nothing when her man, the man she loved, was still fighting for his life.

Amara made a long wolf howl, calling for Runo, her best friend, 'Auuuuu, auuuu,' she howled, lifting her chin up, just as the wolves would do to call upon one another in times of danger. 'Auuuuu, auuuu,' she continued.

'Ohhh hey, I am here, no need to be so loud!' said Runo standing right next to her and staring at her with his magic big eyes, one blue and one green which had always amazed her in their beauty, 'I am at your service my lady Amara,' he continued.

'Runo! I need your help, Rupert is in huge danger. He is still fighting Henri and his army so we need to go and help him,' she replied and pointed towards the burning castle which was visible in the distance.

'Your wish is my command, you know I would do anything for you,' replied Runo and made the most terrifying howl that Amara had ever heard in her life, 'Auuuuuuuuuu,' he howled and all the wolves of the forest replied; 'Auuuuuuuuuu,' gathering together and running towards him, knowing it was the call for help and a call for war. They were always there to support one another in times like this and this was their call for action.

'Here, look at your forest army Amara,' said Runo pointing at hundreds of wolves at their feet, bowing towards them, showing their loyalty and readiness for the battle.

Amara then heard another loud noise all around her and when she turned around she saw all the male deer emerging from the darkness. Their antlers were burning with a blue glowing fire and illuminated the whole forest. There were hundreds of them. She knew that she had the whole forest to help her now.

'We are reporting for duty,' she heard a tiny voice right behind her and when she looked down she saw Emily wearing a wooden pot with a handle sticking to the left, holding a frying pan made of wood in her right paw. Behind her, there were hundreds of other badgers dressed in such armour, exactly the same. 'Mama Badger Army is ready for the battle,' added Emily.

'You will be fighting with, with frying pans?' asked Amara, amused by the unexpected but the cutest sight that melted her heart and seeing the bravery of them all.

'Yes we will, you have no idea how deadly the frying pan can be for a naughty husband,' replied Emily with a gleaming smile.

'Oh, you have used it on your husbands?'

'Well, no, at least I haven't yet. Mine ran away and hid in the rabbit hole as soon as he had seen me once like this at the door when he came back three days after the swan bachelor party. He didn't leave that hole for four days and even today when I see the rabbit babies I sometimes wonder why they have badger teeth when they smile at me coming back from the river school each day,' she replied.

'Ok, well in that case, let's go!' exclaimed Amara and jumped on Runo's back making a long howl and ready for the battle.

'Auuuuuu,' she howled and just as Runo set off and started running, she grabbed the helmet of one of Henri's knights lying on the ground, put it on, and when she saw the giant eagle's white feathers by the ferns, she took a bunch of them and tucked them at the back of the helmet. She then lifted the long silver sword that was stuck in the ground and pointed it towards the sky. The deer, the wolves, and the badgers followed her into the battle of a lifetime.

'We need to help Rupert, we will fight for him!' exclaimed Amara with fierce confidence feeling the cold wind on her face, the branches hurting her face and bare arms but all she knew was that she was never going to leave Rupert alone. She had to fight. She had to show him how much she cared about him.

When they approached the castle on fire, the battle was still on, the trees were lying on the ground with their branches cut off, unable to move and fight, many of Henri's knights were also lying on the ground covered in blood, squashed by the trees that had fallen onto them. Amara was so angry seeing so much pain, suffering, and destruction in her beloved forest that she made a loud howl; 'Auuuuuuuuu! Let's fight for Rupert!' and all the animals followed her. Her sword was cutting through the armour of the cruel men at a lightning speed.

Runo was carrying her closer and closer to the fighting men and trees but at the same time, he was getting more and more wounded by the swords cutting through his thick fur. When Amara felt as if she was lifted high up in the air, she looked up and saw the white giant eagle that had grabbed her leather corset straps at the back giving her its wings to fly. Runo looked at her from down below but she only smiled at him. He could now tear the heads off the evil knights without worrying about Amara on his back and she was now an indestructible woman with wings of an eagle which flew her closer from one knight to another and helped her navigate through them, cutting their arms and heads off until warm blood was gushing high up in the air, only just missing Amara. Whenever it could, the eagle used its large red beak to rip their eyes out so she could fight them more easily. The giant white eagle became part of her now because she was the one who could defeat the evil army of Prince Henri.

She noticed Rupert fighting with the last remains of his branches but he seemed to have been losing being tied up with ropes from all directions by men who tried to pull him into the ground. She pointed the eagle in his direction and immediately cut off all the ropes holding Rupert. She then slashed all the heads of the knights who were holding them and her eagle ripped their eyes out once their helmets were off.

'Rupert! Run, I shall find you! Run to our secret spot by the river!' she exclaimed just as she had been put onto the ground by the eagle who flew away seeing that the battle was over now. Henri was lying unconscious in mud and unable to hurt them anymore but Amara wanted to be sure that he wouldn't.

'Please, Rupert, go, just go!' she exclaimed, and seeing his teary eyes she felt like crying too but she knew she had to be strong, 'they will not stop this until they have killed you. Please, just go and wait for me there!' she added with a calm and loving voice.

'Please come to me as soon as you can,' he replied with a low and weak voice, moving away slowly burnt, hurt, with no branches and with hardly any energy left.

Amara walked up to Henri and touched his arm but he did not move.

'Let's retreat!' she shouted to all the deer with antlers piercing the knights' armour in all the places possible, setting them on fire and mama badgers hitting their helmets with frying pans with a loud bang and making sure they wouldn't ever get up again.

Amara didn't want any more of the animals and trees to be hurt in this battle. She jumped on Runo's back. His teeth were now covered in blood and his silver fur was badly cut and bleeding from the swords. His white heart shape on his silver fur also looked as if it was bleeding. Amara touched it to stop the blood from flowing. Her forest army followed her back, proud to have fought together for Rupert.

'I order you to cut every oak in this forest before dusk! Do you understand me?' Henri exclaimed to his guard right next to him, the Commander in Chief of Fardom, as soon as he had regained consciousness and stood up swaying from side to side.

'Every oak my lord?' the man repeated with hesitation in his voice because he knew it would lead to almost all trees of the forest gone.

'Yes! Every single oak! I want all of them gone. Especially Rupert. He has to die. Do you understand me?' Henri exclaimed angrily, removing mud from his armour.

'I do, my Lord.'

Chapter 27

CROSSROADS

Rupert was moving slowly and following the moonlight which illuminated his path.

He was weak and badly wounded. He just wanted to be close to Amara again. He stopped at the crossroads of two paths leading in opposite directions. He was so exhausted from the battle that he couldn't remember seeing this spot before and which path was actually leading to the riverbank, his and Amara's home since they had met.

'Which is the right one?' he wondered.

'Only you know which path is the right one for you,' he heard the voice of the Moon shining bright above him.

'I know? How do I know?' he mumbled.

'Yes, you already know which path is the right one for you. Deep in your heart and soul. You know which one to choose. You see, each path could be right for you and each can be bad for you too. That's because each of them has both the good and the bad in it. The most important thing for you is to know and accept the fact that with each choice that you may think is right for you, there is ultimately a sacrifice you need to make. Because that's what life is all about. Choices and accepting what is. Now and forever. Nothing will ever be perfect. But everything can be perfect for you when you accept both the good and the bad,' replied the Moon in a warm loving voice.

'I, I think I wanted to go to the right,' Rupert mumbled trying to follow the Moon's advice, 'is it the right path?' he asked but when he looked up the Moon was already hidden behind white clouds and darkness had fallen upon both paths.

Following the one on the right, he noticed that the forest was getting denser and denser, making it harder and harder for him to move. The giant ferns were getting more and more vicious, blocking his path and holding onto his roots when he started to lose balance. Suddenly he felt his roots sinking into the wet ground as if he was drowning in a swamp. The ivy was quickly wrapping around him, making it hard for him to breathe as if it wanted to suffocate him.

'Oh, no, what's happening? I can't move. Where am I?' he said to himself, petrified at the thought of being stuck in the wet ground which he didn't remember was even there, and not being able to make it to the river as a meeting spot with Amara. 'What is she going to think now? That I abandoned her? That I ran away and left her?' he thought to his horror.

'Don't worry, it's only the beginning of the end,' he heard a petrifying voice of a woman that he had once heard before, 'you didn't think I would just let you live happily ever after with Amara, even as a tree, did you?' the voice continued and when he looked around he saw the same old man in a hood that had appeared in front of him when he turned into an oak.

'Oh, it's you,' he said confused, 'what's wrong with your voice?'

'Don't you recognise me Rupi? It's me,' he heard Forest

Mother's voice, and looking closely at the old man he watched him transform into her.

'It's, it's you?' he gasped in disbelief at what he had just witnessed.

'Yes, it's me you fool, what did you expect? Fairy godmother?' replied Forest Mother laughing in a voice of a madwoman, 'yes, it was me all along, you just never saw it. I told you when you rejected me that you shall stay in this forest as a tree forever as a punishment and I shall keep my word. You are going nowhere now. You cannot escape your destiny. It's only a matter of hours or even minutes before you will be cut in half by Henri's men.'

'Why are you doing this to me? Why are you so cruel to me?' Rupert asked in despair.

'Because I offered you true love, my true love, but you preferred that stupid Amara,' she replied and swooshed her long green coat with a large swing towards her whilst moving closer to Rupert.

'I told you I don't love you, I only love Amara and she is not stupid. She is the most wonderful, loving, and caring woman on Earth. Unlike you!' he exclaimed angrily, knowing that speaking his truth would not harm him anymore.

'I gave you a chance,' she said and touched his bark but he only swayed an inch away from her, 'anyway, it was nice to know you, after all, you should be happy I didn't turn you into another chair,' she added and swiftly turned around merging into one of the oaks in front of him and appearing on the other side of it. Her skin had a green undertone in the moonlight which was now shining back upon them and Rupert even thought that parts of it looked like tree bark.

'You are, you are not Forest Mother, you are a dryad!' he exclaimed to his shock.

'Yes, I am a dryad you fool. But I am the queen of all dryads and all living creatures in this forest, including you,' she replied in a mad voice, 'I can command anything I want from all the animals, plants, and trees. I can do anything I want and other dryads do what I wish to. It's only because of you all of them will die with their oaks now. Look what you have done idiot. You have caused this slaughter to this forest only because you love that silly Amara.'

'It's not my fault! Don't blame me for something you have caused! Yes, you are right, you are no Forest Mother. Forest Mother would love all the living creatures and trees. You are pure evil that tried to force me to love you.'

'I only wanted you as my love slave that's all. Is that too much to ask for when you are alone in the forest and have no oak tree that would have me as his? I only did it because I wanted to be.. loved.'

'Well, you will never find love when you act with revenge, magic spells, and wickedness. That's not love,' replied Rupert, starting to feel a bit of compassion for her for the first time.

'I shall find my true love no matter what and no matter with what human. Nobody will stop me. Not even you,' she announced and disappeared, leaving Rupert all alone.

All he could hear now was the petrifying noise of the trees being cut by Henri's guards, getting closer and closer.

'I love you Amara,' he whispered to the Moon, hoping for it to give the message to the one and only woman he had ever loved.

***

'When I felt each blow of a sharp axe cutting deep into my trunk I felt more and more at peace with myself. After all, I got to live two lives in this lifetime. One of a human and one of a tree. Who can ever say that?

But the biggest pain in my soul was because I had never listened to Amara and that I disappointed her in every possible way. That I never showed her the ultimate unconditional love that she deserves and I have always felt for her because I was driven by my big ego, thinking that Forest Mother could take the spell away but I was wrong. Well, she could take it away but who would have thought she never would because of her own egotistical intentions of forcing me to love her? And if I did choose to be a human again, Amara would die. We all seem to have our own mission in life and sometimes our missions can clash with one another in the most unexpected and unusual ways. Forest Mother had her mission. I had mine.

Each blow of the axe felt like a punishment for everything I had done wrong in my life and mainly during my time as a tree. With every blow, I also knew that my mission still wasn't complete in this lifetime, neither as a human nor as a tree. But then why would trees be allowed to have and complete any missions in life? We are considered by humans to be stupid and soulless, even though we have seen and experienced more than any human can imagine.

I am so sorry Amara. I just wish I could tell you that and how much I truly love you. I love you so much that I chose to stay as a tree for you so that you can live.'

I started to lose my balance. The group of four strong men seemed to be doing a good job, cutting really deep into my flesh, ripping out my heart and soul.

I swayed to the side.

'Attention!' the tallest man shouted to the others standing by my side, 'almost there!'

I was calm, even though I wanted to scream: How dare you? Don't you know who I am? Stop right now! But there was no point in me even trying to say that. They would have never heard me. They would have never stopped.

I just wished, I just wished I could see Amara for the last time before I died. I so wanted to tell her so many things and squeeze her till I scratch her soft and fragile skin. I just wish I could say goodbye to my love but she was nowhere to be found. I was alone and I had to be brave even in my darkest hour, even facing certain death. I looked down and I was already cut into half of my trunk. The men looked tired and stopped, drinking water from the jars they had brought with them. I knew that the end was close and that my suffering was about to end. I was about to see the darkness or maybe the light. I was about to experience what it was like to be... dead.

I suddenly saw a woodpecker sitting on the opposite tree and watching me with tears in his eyes.

'Hey! Can you do something for me?' I asked.

'Me??' he replied with a surprise in his voice.

'Yes, you! Could you carve out something on me? A Message for someone, someone I love?'

'Now?'

'Yes, now.'

'Ok, what would you like me to carve out?'

'I think you know the answer to that,' I replied and whispered into his, well the area where his ear would be, not far from his beak. He got to work immediately

'Just hurry, please!' I said to him, knowing that my end was imminent and could happen at any time.

Knowing that my final message to Amara was just being carved into the bark I felt a heightened sense of peace. I could die now knowing that what I wanted to tell her will stay carved into me forever. I just hoped she could see it before they cut me into more pieces.

She was so right about Forest Mother. She was never meant to save me. She was never meant to help me. She was a horrible egotistical witch.

'Egotistical witch?' I heard her voice and when I looked down I saw her standing right in front of me, mounted on a giant wolf that did not look friendly to me at all.

His white, sharp teeth were gleaming at the moonlight. He was growling loudly and saliva was dripping on both sides of his terrifying jaws.

'I was hoping for some remorse Rupert,' she continued, 'I was hoping for….. you changing your mind…' she added with a terrifying look in her eyes.

'How dare you show up here now? At the hour of my death and still lecture me?' I replied, furious to see her cold, pale face with no emotion or compassion for me, 'You wanted to force me to love you and because your horrible cruel plan didn't work you decided to kill me. You are a heartless, merciless woman and all I can feel towards you now is a pity.'

'Pity?' she shouted with fury.

'Yes, pity!' I repeated confidently, 'you do not care about anyone or anything that surrounds you. You are not the loving Forest Mother you are pretending to be. You are evil. Pure evil and sooner or later everyone who serves you will realise it and karma will have no mercy upon you. Your wicked spells will have no powers anymore and you will vanish into the darkness, forgotten forever and ever, without leaving a positive mark on this world. You will become a legend but a legend that will warn others for centuries to come that evil never wins and love always does.'

'Love always wins? Really?' she said laughing loudly and with clear contempt, 'if love always wins where is your true love now? Where is she? Why isn't she helping you?'

'She is my true love and I know it and you know it!'

'Oh, is she now?? A tree dryad who doesn't even know who she is... is your true love?'

'Yes.'

'Well, why doesn't she care about your death now? Maybe because she is enjoying her life with her TRUE LOVE, Prince Henri?'

'Nooo, he is not her true love. She is alone now because of me, because I rejected her and because I told her to go away.'

'Ohh poor Rupi, and you think anybody cares about this now? Do you think anybody cares about your death? You are one of the millions of trees in this forest, you are one of them now and nobody cares if you are cut down or not. Nobody except me of course. If only you had said a word, if only you said you truly love me, I would save you. So, do you Rupert? Do you love me and want to be with me forever?'

'Nooooo,' he shouted back immediately, 'I do not and I never will! I prefer to die and be cut into millions of pieces than to be with you!'

'What??? You prefer death to an eternity of happiness with me and my perfect body?'

'Yes!' I replied with more confidence as a dying tree than one can imagine.

If only it was Amara who was asking me the same question. I knew that nothing and nobody was going to save me now. I knew I was about to... My thoughts started to disappear into the darkness of the sky above my head. I lost my balance and I fell. I... was... deeee......

Chapter 28

THE END IS THE BEGINNING

When Amara approached the riverside at twilight the next day having spent hours searching for Rupert, she didn't know that what she was about to witness was going to be a sight to remember forever, and not in a good way.

'Rupert!! Rupert!! Where are you?' she shouted with full force in her lungs before she noticed a massive tree lying flat on the ground.

The stars were only appearing one after another in the sky so she couldn't see its leaves which would tell her what tree it was. When she got even closer, however, she could clearly see that it was... an oak tree.

'Oh no!' she exclaimed in a crying voice which would wake the dead, 'this cannot be you!' she added when she stopped right by the side of the trunk.

It was quiet. There was nobody around. All she could hear was the crickets in the ferns and frogs by the riverside. She approached it even closer, so close she could touch the dark brown bark, burnt from the fire. Seeing many of the branches cut off she asked in a breaking voice; 'Is this you Rupert? Am I too late?'

On the side of the trunk she noticed a carving in the shape of a heart which said; Rupert + Amara = True Love.

She knew it was him, the man who was the love of her life. And she also knew that she had lost him FOREVER. She closed her eyes and big tears fell down her cheeks like a waterfall.

'I am so sorry, I am sorry I am late,' she whispered, choking through her tears..

She fell lifeless with her arms wrapping the trunk and let her tears fall from her dark eyes like logs kidnapped by the strong current of a river. She did not even try to stop them. She would not be able to anyway.

'I'm sorry I didn't find you before. I'm sorry I left and abandoned you for the shallow and narcissistic Prince Henri. I would have never done it if you hadn't rejected me. Why did you do it, Rupert? Why did you tell me to go away and why did you tell me to go to hell when Heaven was right here with us?' she screamed in despair knowing that the love of her life died and there was nothing she could do about it.

She could not save him now.

All her forest friends gathered around her and Rupert in silence, watching them with tearful eyes; Robin, badger families with their babies, squirrel Leticia, mandarin duck, Olek, and deer with blue glowing antlers.

'What are you doing here?' she asked through her tears, 'you are not meant to be here! This is not a show and this is not a funeral. Rupert is not dead! He is alive! He will always be in my heart and soul. He is and always will be the love of my life,' she continued standing up proudly making the speech of her life, 'This man, Rupert is the man who loved me and I love him with my whole heart. He is not dead. He is part of this forest now. He is part of the Universe. He is part of us. He is part of you and me... do you hear me? He is not dead. Don't you dare feel sad or sorry for him or me. He is alive... among us... just in a different form. I was not here on time to tell him how much I love him and that I chose him regardless of his weirdness of being an oak. I was too late. But I say it aloud right now. I say it to you; RUPERT IS THE PRINCE TO BE REMEMBERED; he is a truly loving and caring gentleman and I want you all to pay respect to him. Now go away!' she said with huge confidence in her voice despite the pain in her heart which was so huge that it could easily kill her now.

All the animals looked at her with big, teary eyes and none of them dared to say anything. But nobody moved either. Amara fell once more with her whole body on the side of the tree, hugging it with her arms, and started weeping, knowing that the flood of tears couldn't be stopped and that she didn't care about what others might say.

'I love you so much, Rupert... I love you when you squeeze me till you scratch me with your branches, I love you till you almost poison me with red mushrooms. I love you to the stars above and back. I love you to the centre of the Earth and more. I love you for your cheeky smile on your huba and for your caring nature. I love you for hiding me in the cave when you get hit by lightning, I love you for keeping me safe on the river bank when you are kidnapped by the river current. I love you for all that you are and all that you have been and would have been for me... you are my hero, my one and only true love, my tree love.'

While Amara was keeping her head on Rupert's dead body, Prince Henri emerged from the ferns with his entourage of angry beasts. He was smiling, seemed proud of himself, and satisfied that he had achieved his goal of killing Rupert. The wolves around him were growling at all the animals gathered around Rupert and Amara, ready for an attack as if they had no soul, no feeling of any compassion for what had happened.

'How could you be so cruel?' asked Amara standing up and looking into Henri's vicious eyes, 'How can you be so happy about Rupert's death? How?' she kept asking, getting closer and closer to him still mounted on the horse, 'You really are a monster. You have no good feelings in you, do you? You are all about hatred and revenge. That's what drives you, doesn't it?' she continued, 'It just makes me really wonder; why? Why have you turned into this horrible human being? But maybe it's too late for me to even ask that. Some people are just cruel, just like you and the reasons are irrelevant. You are who you are. But all I can say to that is that I feel sorry for you. You must be truly an unhappy man to live by such low standards and values. You wish bad upon others and you think it will be without any consequences. But I have news for you. This Universe is fair. This Universe is ruled by love not hatred and love always wins,' she added with confidence that this forest had never seen.

She then turned towards the wild beasts by his side who were showing their angry teeth dripping with saliva, ready for an attack as soon as she or any of her animal companions made a wrong move.

'You don't need to be like this. You don't need to be evil. I know who you truly are. You are creatures of this forest. And this forest is pure love. So you must be love too. You have forgotten about it being under the spell of this wicked man. But I believe in you. I believe in the goodness of your soul. Trust me when I say; I love you and I always will. For you are my friends and you shall be forever,' she said and the wild beasts hid their white teeth, stopped making sounds, and stared at Amara with their big eyes as if hypnotised. 'I love you,' she repeated and at that moment, all of them bowed to her making an apologetic sound as if they had woken up from a nightmare.

'Oh, I can see what you did there!' exclaimed Henri from his horse having realised he had now lost all his beasts, 'you think you have won. You haven't. I still have a sword and I can kill...' he added, taking his sword out and aiming at Amara's head but in the very same moment, all the beasts jumped onto him, throwing off his horse and tearing his body into pieces.

Amara opened her eyes as she had thought he would have killed her with one blow of his sword and couldn't see much of Henri's body left. The beasts didn't even leave much for the hyenas who were always eager to help in moments like this.

She then felt as if she was falling into a deep sleep, getting weaker and weaker as if she was about to die herself. She lay her fainting body on the trunk, closed her eyes, and surrendered, allowing it to just be. She let the feeling take control. She was becoming motionless, powerless, and ready to die.

'What is happening to me?' she thought, squeezing Rupert's dead body more and more, gazing at the stars covering the dark sky with a million sparkles.

'Where are you, Rupert? Are you one of them now? Are you a star now?' she whispered, drowning into the darkness of the biggest pain of her life, 'thank you for being part of my existence. Thank you for being part of my story,' she added with the last remains of her strength, 'YOU ARE THE TRUE LOVE I HAVE BEEN SEARCHING FOR ALL MY LIFE,' she said and closed her eyes, ready to surrender to the Universe, 'I LOVE YOU.'

At that moment, hundreds of butterflies pulsating with blue

glowing light wrapped Rupert and Amara, blinding all the animals who were stunned at this magical scene.

'I LOVE YOU TOO' Amara heard a familiar voice and when she opened her eyes she saw Rupert's eyes lovingly sparking in the moonlight.

'You are alive! You are truly alive!'

'Yes my love and so are you,' Rupert replied and slowly lifted himself up, looking powerful and strong with his branches and leaves back as if nothing had ever happened.

'You.. you are...'

'Yes, I am alive thanks to you, thanks to your true love for me,' he replied, watching her with soft teary eyes.

'But how...?'

'How? Well, you are part of me... and I am part of you... forever, for as long as one of us lives... we can save each other from death.'

'Really? I am so happy. I am so sorry Ru...'

'Shhh...'

'Do you forgive me?' she asked.

'Do I forgive you?? What do you want me to forgive you for? You are forgiveness, you are love and you are compassion already. You are also my dryad and you shall live for as long as I live, meaning for a thousand years and more. I hope it's good news to you?' he added with a gentle loving smile.

'I am a... dryad?' she asked with a clear surprise in her voice.

'Yes... my dryad. It's all because of the wicked Forest Mother. But she will not hurt you or me anymore. I can guarantee you that. You saved me because you truly loved me and now I shall live for you because I love you. I chose to stay an oak because

I want to love you forever,' he said, lifting her up with two of his newly reborn branches.

'You chose to be a tree? Does it mean you sacrificed your life as a prince to be with me?'

'Love is not a sacrifice. Love is a choice. And I could not have chosen otherwise. Living as a prince but losing you would mean eternal death to my soul. How could I betray my soul? And I want to live and share my love with you forever and ever,' he replied, swirling Amara around in the joyful dance.

'They say love does not last FOREVER but would five thousand years make you happy?? If I was able to live that long and it is possible considering my current circumstances, would you love me as much as I love you, for five thousand years? And if I could love you for ten thousand years, would you love me too? What if I could love you FOREVER and EVER, even if I die, even if they cut me into pieces and make a table from me, would you still love me? Would you?'

'Of course, I would. I will love you till the end of the Universe and back,' replied Amara hugging him tightly.

All the gathered animals cheered and clapped with whatever they could; their paws, their hoofs, their frog legs, and Robin kept repeating; 'Quack me. Now that's a story!'

'I truly am part of you and you are part of me, forever and ever!' exclaimed Amara and stretched her arms, even more, wrapping around Rupert and slowly disappearing into his bark. Millions of fireflies surrounded Rupert in a dance of eternal passion of the light of love.

'Well, well, well,' everyone heard the low, scary voice of Forest Mother who had come to the scene on a silver beast.

'You have lost. Go away and leave us in peace. Our love has won and there is nothing you can do about it,' said Rupert holding Amara to the side.

'You fool! You think I have lost? You are wrong. I have not and you both shall pay for your stupidity and being stubborn!' she screamed and lifted her arm holding her long wooden stick as if trying to get all the evil forces to come along and demolish the world order.

Rupert, seeing what was about to happen, hit her with full force. She hit her head on the ground and lost consciousness but the battle had only begun. The beast opened its jaws showing off its giant teeth dripping with saliva, growling at Rupert, ready to attack. Rupert with only a few moves of his branches threw him high up into the air. He fell onto the ground with a big thump making a squeak.

'Noooo! Stop! It's Runo!' exclaimed Amara having recognised her beloved friend and walked up to him, lying on the ground badly hurt now, scowling from pain.

'Runo, it's me, Amara. Your best friend remember?' she asked, touching his silver fur on his head gently. He was staring into her eyes as if confused.

'I love you Runo, and I know you love me,' she whispered into his big ears which were shaped into a triangle, just like every time he was naughty or wanted to play. I love you,' she kept repeating and Runo was getting calmer and calmer as if falling asleep, 'You have been under the spell of this wicked Forest Mother but you are with me now, safe,' she continued and touched the white heart engraved in his silver fur as if trying to connect to his real heart.

It worked. Runo stood up and licked her face, wanting cuddles.

'Oh, you are back my darling!' said Amara in a joyful voice, hugging and kissing him.

Rupert looked at Forest Mother who was lying on the ground, stunned at the scene. When she opened her mouth, spiders, big as a bear's fist, that followed her as her servants, crawled on top of her body, swiftly weaving their nets all over her and soon turned her into a giant cocoon. The wolves that used to be under Henri's spell then ripped her into pieces and any remains of her turned into cockroaches running around the deer's feet. They stepped on them and seeing that every piece of her flesh turned into a new cockroach, the deer started jumping up and down. Each cockroach was stepped upon and the only thing that was left of her was splashes of their disgusting bodies. Karma had reached both Henri and Forest Mother. They both died from a death that they had deserved for how they had lived their lives. Because karma reaches everyone. Good and bad. We all have to bear the consequences of our actions.

'My friends. This is only the beginning. The beginning of happy times in this forest. Nobody shall suffer or be subject to the manipulations of this witch who had called herself Forest Mother. We are free now to live in peace, harmony, and love. We shall continue to do so. Love and justice always win. The Universe loves and protects us, the Universe is part of us and we are part of the Universe. We are nature, we are the good and the peace that brings this physical existence together. Together we can live, love and exist. Together, forever we shall protect what we have so that our children and their children learn to love and appreciate. Thank you all for showing me what being part of YOU truly means. Thank you for helping me to find out what true love really means. Love is within us all, love is you in you, Robin, love is in you mama badger, love is in you Runo, love is in you Amara, love is in me, an old but young oak. Love is all there is. It is the most powerful force in the Universe and it shall always win!' said Rupert, proud of all the lessons he had learnt from his tree existence.

All the animals cheered and danced to the sweetest songs played by the crickets and frogs, hugged and kissed the trees and the whole forest celebrated the victory of love over evil.

The fireflies together with glowing blue butterflies flew high up to the starry sky and everyone watched them writing a message for the rest of the world which said:

FIND

TREE

LOVE

EPILOGUE

Rupert and Amara finally united forever and their love became eternal.

Rupert accepted who he was and loved himself as a tree, the surrounding nature, and the Universe, knowing that it was the only way to live a happy life while loving Amara with eternal, unconditional love. Eternal, meaning always being together, forever and ever. You must know that Rupert and Amara still live now. Locals of the ancient magical forest, which is now Windsor Great Park, often see their silhouettes embracing lovingly in the middle of the biggest oak. Their love is truly everlasting because it has already lasted over five hundred years and it is one that will be remembered forever. Because true love always wins after all. The eternal love that we as humans are always searching for but rarely find. Next time you visit Windsor Great Park make sure to find Rupert the oak and his dryad Amara. Hug it. Feel its energy and enjoy their love for you. They say that everyone who hugs Rupert and Amara's oak will also find eternal love in their human existence.

Tourists from all over the world can often swear on their own life that they see shadows of Rupert and Amara's humanlike silhouettes running and dancing among the trees, merging into the turquoise depths of the Virginia Water waterfall, hugging and kissing on its surface, gently pulling each other in all directions but never leaving each other's embrace and a touch of their hands, melting into the lake and disappearing in it, blending with the ripples shimmering in the setting sun at twilight. Their laughs echo from the rocks and dissolve in the far distance of the valleys. Some say that they also see someone else with them; the silhouette of the most beautiful dark-haired girl one could imagine, giggling in the sweetest voice, playing with the ducklings on the shore, and following them into the lake to bathe with them.

The shadows Rupert, Amara, and their daughter's silhouettes always shine in what the watchers call 'the eternal light of love', an aura of colourful rainbows around them radiating with an unearthly joy and bliss, as if they lived their lives together in a perfect harmony that everyone wants to find, if one could call it living of course. They are now the spirits of the forest and they will live forever as long as they have their forest, their heaven on Earth to dwell in.

Recently, one of the tourists has looked at a humongous oak tree near the Copper Horse statue of George IV and he swears he could see their happy faces, smiling at him, living in that tree. Amara was hugging Rupert's strong body really tightly as if they have never separated all this time and just as the tourist wanted to take a picture, they both melted into its bark. A chill went down his spine letting him know that it was not a sight to take a picture of. But locals to Windsor say that Rupert and Amara are happy to share their love with anyone who desires it and if you really want to feel their love, you just need to hug their oak, close your eyes, let the sun rays and gentle breeze penetrate your skin wrapping each strand of your hair, breathe in deeply and let tears fill your eyes. You shall then see a glimpse of Heaven, the true paradise of nature.

Windsorians also say that the daughter's name is Driana. They heard that name whispered in their ears many times during their walks in the park. They claim she is now a dazzling beauty with chestnut hair and porcelain skin that sometimes shimmers at moonlight and turns slightly green in the morning sunlight. She runs around the oaks looking a little lost, perhaps searching for her own place on Earth, dressed in only oak leaves around her waist and a necklace made of acorns covering her breasts. She wears a flower crown made of bluebells and jasmine so when she passes them by, they can smell the intoxicating scent, leaving them, especially men partially hypnotised. Windsorians, therefore, warn all single men not to go to Windsor Great Park alone because Driana, according to the legend, still hasn't found true love for over five hundred years, supposedly wanting to find love that is as deep and everlasting as that of her parents, Rupert and Amara. As a result, men may find themselves seduced by her and kept captive as her 'love slave' because that's what dryads can do if they wish to. But you probably know what it is like with legends. Only some are actually true. Rupert and Amara shall live forever, bathing in their deep, true, everlasting, and eternal love because their destiny was always about Finding Tree Love.

You will find it too.
But only if you wish to search for it.
It is there.
Deep in your heart and soul.
Because TRUE love is a choice.

So is TREE love.

I am no princess.

You are no prince.

But let's be happy with who we truly are.

You are everything I could ever dream of.

You are part of me

And I am part of you.

We are one when we become one.

We are love.

We can all find it.

When we FIND TREE LOVE.

THE END

www.ingramcontent.com/pod-product-compliance
Lightning Source LLC
Chambersburg PA
CBHW070943180726
48291CB00004B/1110